THE URBANA FREE LIBRARY

47

D1310655

URBANA FREE LIBRARY

	DATE DUE		

The Urbana Free Library

To renew materials call
217-367-4057

On a Medieval Day

Story Voyages Around the World

Rona Arato

Illustrated by Peter Ferguson

MAPLE TREE PRESS

5|11
18⁰⁰

Maple Tree Press books are published by Owlkids Books Inc.
10 Lower Spadina Avenue, Suite 400, Toronto, Ontario M5V 2Z2
www.owlkids.com

Text © 2010 Rona Arato
Illustrations © 2010 Peter Ferguson

All rights reserved. No part of this book may be reproduced or copied in any form
without written consent from the publisher.

Distributed in Canada by Raincoast Books
9050 Shaughnessy Street, Vancouver, British Columbia V6P 6E5

Distributed in the United States by Publishers Group West
1700 Fourth Street, Berkeley, California 94710

Library and Archives Canada Cataloguing in Publication

Arato, Rona
        On a medieval day : story voyages around the world
 / Rona Arato ; illustrated by Peter Ferguson ; [maps and
spot illustrations, Colin McGill].

ISBN 978-1-897349-94-6 (bound).--ISBN 978-1-897349-95-3 (pbk.)

        1. Middle Ages--Juvenile fiction.
I. Ferguson, Peter, 1968- II. McGill, Colin III. Title.

PS8601.R35O56 2010   jC813'.6   C2010-900319-5

Library of Congress Control Number: 2010920480

Design: Samantha Edwards

 Canada Council   Conseil des Arts    ONTARIO ARTS COUNCIL
for the Arts   du Canada   CONSEIL DES ARTS DE L'ONTARIO
We acknowledge the financial support of the Canada Council for the Arts, the Ontario Arts Council,
the Government of Canada through the Canada Book Fund (CBF), and the Government of Ontario
through the Ontario Media Development Corporation's Book Initiative for our publishing activities.

Manufactured by WKT Co. Ltd.
Manufactured in Shenzhen, Guangdong, China in April 2010.
Job # 09CB4477

A   B   C   D   E   F

Publisher of Chirp, chickaDEE and OWL
www.owlkids.com

Contents

To Sheba and Anne, with thanks.
—Rona

Dear Reader,

On a Medieval Day covers a period in history that lasted from about the 400s to the 1400s. During this time, around the world there were great differences in people's lifestyles. In Europe, most people were illiterate. The Catholic Church was the strongest group and only priests, monks, and nobility were taught to read. Outbreaks of the plague, a terrible disease also known as the Black Death, killed millions of people. In cities such as Venice, over half the population died.

In Muslim countries, this period is known as the Golden Islamic Age because it was a time when learning and science, such as astronomy, mathematics, and medicine, flourished. Muslim doctors found the cures to many diseases. They discovered the concept of "zero" and started using the numerals (1, 2, 3...) that we use today. China produced art, science, and literature. In Africa, the Mali Empire grew into an important trading center. In what is today Mexico and Guatemala, the Mayas developed a complex civilization and built great cities. This was also a time when the Vikings sailed to the New World— five hundred years before Christopher Columbus!

In this book you will meet nine kids at different times and places during the medieval era. Although they aren't real, their stories and experiences are based on real events and the customs of their time. Their lives are very different, not only from yours, but from each other's. Their experiences will help you understand what a complex period the medieval era was. I hope you enjoy reading their stories as much as I enjoyed writing them.

Rona Arato

A Serious Game

Tikal, Mayan Civilization, 720

Morning

uy could barely contain his excitement. Today was the day of the *pitz* ball game between his cousin Huj's team and a team from the city of Palenque. Both teams were known for their skill and were champions of their region. Kuy wanted to be as good as his cousin and someday play in the ball court in this great city of Tikal.

"Is it not beautiful?" His father, Tuktuk, pointed to the great pyramid of Tikal. It soared into the air; a magnificent structure of stone. "We will return for the ceremonies. But first, we must take our produce to the market."

"And go to the pitz game." Kuy hopped from one foot to another. "I cannot wait to see Huj kill the other team."

"Kuy!" His father gave him a stern look. "Do not speak in terms of killing other players!"

"I did not mean to actually kill them." Kuy looked contrite. "Unless they play like the Hero Twins."

"The Hero Twins! Is that all you can talk about?" His older brother, Kej, laughed. "It is time for you to grow up, Kuy. Huj is playing for Tikal."

"As will I someday."

"If you want to be a great player you must first learn how to hit the ball," Kej teased. "Then I will teach you to make your own ball. It is an art that every great player should know well."

Kuy fumed. Kej, who was fourteen, could make him feel like a baby, even though there were only two years between them. Kej was the best ball player in their village. He could dart around the taller players and connect with the ball before they knew where it had gone. And he had mastered the art of mixing sap from the rubber tree with liquid from morning glory plants to make a soft bouncy substance that he formed into a ball.

"Boys, we must sell our wares before the game." Kuy's mother, Mayal, set her basket on the ground and fixed her eyes, dark and serious, on them.

It was more than a sport; it was a sacred ritual...

Kuy rubbed his eyes. He was sleepy. It was a two-day walk from their village to the city. They had spent the night at a way station. Rising before dawn, they had eaten a breakfast of corn dough diluted with water from a nearby stream. Before leaving home they had put the dough, which they mixed with spices and chili, into pouches. They wore bowl-shaped gourds on their heads and used them as dishes to eat the corn mixture. At home they added squash, vegetables, and meat to their corn-based diet.

After breakfast, they had joined the crowd of people on the road who were going to the great city. Today was the twentieth day of the month, when a religious festival was held. During the ceremonies later that day the priests would climb the pyramid steps. They would wear huge headdresses and fierce masks and perform rites to please the gods. This was important, Kuy knew, because if the God of Rain or the God of Maize were unhappy, the crops would not grow and people would starve.

Kuy followed his parents to the market where dozens of people were offering their wares for sale. They found a clear space and set down the baskets. In addition to maize, Mayal had brought bolts of brightly decorated cotton cloth that she had woven. Her loose-fitting dress was made from the same cotton as the *ex*, the loincloth the men wore. Tuktuk was selling Godpots, wooden bowls used for *copal*, a type of incense that was burned to feed the gods. Some of the merchandise would be traded for other goods and some sold for cocoa beans, which were highly prized as both a condiment added to food and a form of money.

While he went through the motions of selling his family's wares, Kuy thought about the game. It was more than a sport; it was a sacred ritual and Kuy knew that people, especially the priests, took it very seriously.

Afternoon

The pitz court was crowded when Kuy, Tuktuk, and Kej arrived. They had sold their corn and their father's pots. Their mother had sold her cloth to a noblewoman and had remained behind to shop and gossip with the other women. Kuy, Kej, and their father took seats on the side of the temple, looking down on the court. Kuy studied the spectators. There were nobles and common people, men and women, all looking forward to an exciting afternoon.

The ball court was built of cut stone painted in bright colors. It was long and narrow with slanted walls that enclosed the court, and was shaped like an "I" with two end zones. Kuy turned to his father. "Huj is a good player, isn't he?"

"He is the best in Tikal. His father was an exceptional player and Huj has inherited his skill. I hope that Huj wins because I have placed a large bet on him."

Kuy looked at him in surprise. "You never bet on the games."

"I have made an exception." Tuktuk smiled. "I want to buy your mother a piece of jade and for that I will need many cocoa beans."

The crowd roared as the teams marched onto the court. The players, dressed in bright feathered headdresses, jewels, and animal skins, were preceded by drummers. Kuy looked for Huj and spotted him at the head of the home team. His headdress was of blue, yellow, and green feathers and, like the other players, he had painted his body red. The opposing team's bodies were painted black.

The drummers stopped drumming as the priests came onto the field. They, too, wore brilliant headdresses. After the blessings were over, the players removed their ceremonial attire and changed into the protective padding that they would wear for the game. This consisted of thigh, arm, and hip protectors. Each player wore a large fabric yoke around his waist. This garment was used to deflect the ball and to protect his midsection. During the game, players positioned themselves so the ball hit the padded parts of their body. The players used their hips, thighs, and forearms to keep the round rubber ball in motion. They could not touch it with their hands, heads, or feet. The goal was to keep the ball in motion. A team scored when it hit a floor marker. When a player scored, the spectators showered him with their clothing and jewelry.

Once they were dressed, the teams faced each other. Kuy grinned in anticipation. A referee tossed the ball in the air and a player from the Tikal team rushed forward and hit it with his forearm. An opposing player swung around and smashed the ball with his leg. Kuy's head snapped back and forth as he followed the ball's crisscross path up and down the court. Suddenly the ball hit the marker and the crowd roared. It was Tikal's point.

"What will you give Huj when he scores a point?" Kuy turned to his father.

"I have brought a special piece of jewelry, just for that occasion." Tuktuk held up a carved wooden bird. "I made this for Huj. Here." He handed it to his son. "You may reward him."

The game resumed. Kuy watched one player, then another hit the ball while the opposing team maneuvered to take it away. Up, up, up it went as the crowd shouted encouragements. Down it came, only to be stopped by a player's hip or elbow. *Wham!* Off it went toward the marker, then, *whoosh*, back to the other side of the court. Kuy's eyes were strained with following the ball, and his neck hurt from twisting it back and forth as the ball and the players crossed and re-crossed the court. When the drummers signaled it was time for a break, only the Tikal team had scored a point.

"Huj! Huj!" Kuy shouted as his cousin walked toward them.

"Hello, Kuy. Hello, Kej." Huj smiled, exposing sharp teeth that were filed to a point. A piece of jade was inserted into a hole in the front of each front tooth. This piece of jewelry showed his high social status.

Tuktuk stood and looked down at Huj. "Your father would be proud of you."

"I am playing for his memory. That is why I must win."

The drummers signaled that it was time for the next round of the game and Huj returned to the field.

"Ohhhh!" A collective groan rose from the stands. The opposing team had scored a point and then a second point.

Kuy clapped his hand to his head. "No," he moaned. Tikal was now losing. He looked at Huj, whose face was creased into a frown.

"Don't worry, boys." Tuktuk said. "Huj will come through."

Sure enough, Huj was on the move. Sidling between players, he positioned himself so he was in front of the opposing players when they passed the ball toward the marker. Swift as a panther he intercepted the ball with his arm, bounced it onto his hip, kicked it, and sent it spinning into the marker. Point Tikal! The crowd jumped to its feet and many spectators suddenly moved back from the court.

"Where is everyone going?" asked Kuy.

His father laughed. "They do not want to part with their clothing or jewelry to reward Huj." Tuktuk slipped a ring from his finger and tossed it to Huj who caught it and waved his thanks.

The spectators returned and the game continued. Back and forth went the ball, as the players chased it. Kuy tried to follow Huj but it was hard in the crush of fans. Suddenly, Kej jumped to his feet. "Look!" He pointed to the field. Huj had hit the ball with his thigh, sending it spiraling into the air. Kuy followed it as it spun across the field toward the floor marker.

The crowd held its breath as the ball hit the marker. "He did it!" Kuy shouted. Tikal was leading again, 3–2.

The day had become hot. Kuy smelled the sweat of dozens of bodies crammed close together. He felt the pulse of their excitement and the heat of their breath as they shouted encouragement to their favorite players. Since Tikal was the home team, most people were rooting for them, but a fair number had come from the provinces to cheer the opposing team. As the afternoon wore on, the game became intense and the spectators' roars got louder and louder.

"We must be driving the Lords of Death crazy. They hate noise," said Kej.

"Perhaps they will invite us to the Underworld for a game, like the Hero Twins," said Kuy, who never tired of hearing the story of the twin gods.

The crowd was on its feet, gesturing at the players, shouting instructions, and even angry oaths. The opposing team had scored again and the game now stood at 3–3.

"Look," shouted Kuy. Huj was running, darting in between the players until he was blocking two players who were passing the ball back and forth as they moved toward the marker. "He's going to do it!" He pounded Kej on the back. "Huj, Huj, Huj," he chanted.

Only a minute remained. The crowd was frantic. Kuy watched as Huj maneuvered close to the ball, took command, and with a mighty thrust of his leg, sent it careering to the marker.

"He did it! He did it!" Kuy jumped up and down.

On the field, Huj stood in the center of his team, his arms in the air as bystanders showered him with gifts. Kuy added the bird his father gave him to the prizes being thrown at his cousin. "He did it! He won the game." Kuy pounded his brother's arm. He hugged his father and then leaped into the air.

The crowd went silent as the priest came onto the field. The members of the losing team knelt before him.

The priest lifted his heavily plumed head and his eyes swept over the crowd. It seemed to Kuy that no one breathed. As the holy man looked down at the kneeling players, Kuy shivered. To lose a game was to suffer a spiritual death.

"You have lost the battle and, in so doing, have suffered the death of your former selves," intoned the priest. "You will now experience a rebirth that will result in an enlightenment that will help you to lead stronger lives that are in tune with the divine."

The players rose. With lowered heads, they left the field. Now it was the victors' turn. The priest faced them. "In winning this game you have transcended mortality and reached for the divine. You are one with the gods."

The crowd erupted in cheers to the beat of the drummers' drums.

Evening

uy stood at the base of the great pyramid as his father welcomed Huj.

"You played a wonderful game. We are proud of you."

"Thank you, Uncle." Huj turned to Kuy and Kej. "And did you enjoy the game?"

"I was worried for you," said Kuy.

"I wasn't," said Kej. "I knew you would win. Now it is time to celebrate." He turned toward the pyramid where a group of musicians had begun to play. While the drummers drummed, others rattled turtle shells and piped music on clay flutes. Dancers in elaborate costumes swayed and whirled as the beads on their headdresses jingled.

> **"We thank the God of Rain, Lady Rainbow, and the God of Maize, and our most special God of Sun."**

A sudden hush fell over the crowd. The musicians stopped playing and the dancers were stilled as the ruler of Tikal mounted the pyramid. Like all noblemen, his head was long and narrow because it had been pressed between boards when he was a newborn baby.

"Today we celebrate *K'atun*." He pointed to the *stela*, a stone slab that had been erected in front of the pyramid. "On this monument is recorded the deeds of our rulers for the past twenty years. The gods have been good. We thank the God of Rain, Lady Rainbow, the God of Maize, and our most special God of Sun. They give us crops and food. With their blessings, our lives are good."

He signaled to the musicians and the dancers to resume.

Kuy watched the spectacle. Tikal had won the ball game. Huj was a hero and his family had sold all their wares. He looked up at the sky. The sun was a dying ball of fire in the west. Yet, thanks to the gods, it would reappear tomorrow, as strong and bright as ever, ensuring that the crops would always grow.

Kuy turned at a tap on his shoulder.

"Tonight you will sleep at my house," said Huj. "My wife and mother have prepared a feast."

After dinner, the family sat around a fire in front of the house. Above them the sky stretched like a dark jewel-studded blanket.

"That is one of the Hero Twins," said Kuy, pointing to the golden ball of the moon.

"They were great ball players," said his mother. "Before they were born, their father and uncle were killed by the death lords of the underworld who liked to play tricks on people."

"They tricked people into dying," said Kuy.

"They invited the boys to play a ball game in the underworld," said Kej.

"Yes," said Mayal. "Now to get there, the Hero Twins entered a dark cave and then crossed a river of spikes, a river of blood, and finally a river of pus. In the underworld, the Lords of Death gave them challenges. The Hero Twins were very clever though—they fooled the underworld lords and won the ball game. The underworld lords wanted to kill the Hero Twins by burning them in an oven. To trick the lords, the Hero Twins jumped into the burning oven and turned to ash. The Lords of Death threw the boys' ashes into a river but the water brought them back to life. The twins disguised themselves and traveled from village to village performing tricks."

"I know what they could do," said Huj. "They could cut themselves up and then put themselves back together. They could burn down a house and then magically build it up again."

"Soon the Lords of Death heard of them, but did not realize they were the Hero Twins," said Mayal. "They invited them to perform. When the boys reached the underworld, the two most important Lords of Death said, 'Chop us up and put us back together.' But the twins tricked them and did not put them back together. When the other lords saw this, they realized they could not defeat the Hero Twins and surrendered, too. Then the Twins were transformed into the sun and the full moon, and rose up into the sky."

Kuy remained awake after everyone was asleep. He looked up at the orange moon that had once been a Hero Twin and smiled. "One day, I will be as great a player as you were," he said to the moon. "And as good as your brother, the sun, and as my cousin Huj."

He could hardly wait to begin. ∽

The ruins, or remains, of the city of Tikal are found in what is now the country of Guatemala.

Masters of the Americas

THE MAYAN CIVILIZATION

A Mayan calendar

The Mayas had one of the most advanced civilizations in the Americas. They lived in what are now the Central American countries of Mexico, Guatemala, Belize, El Salvador, and western Honduras. Scholars believe the first Mayan civilizations began around 2600 BCE. They built great cities and elaborate pyramids—cutting and moving massive stones—all without the use of metal tools! Some of their cities had populations of more than one hundred thousand people.

The Mayas understood mathematics and astronomy. They tracked time by studying the sun, moon, and the planet Venus. They used two calendars: one was a year with eighteen months of twenty days each—plus five unlucky days; the other was a religious calendar with two hundred and sixty days. Each day of the religious calendar had a name and a number and was linked to a god. The Mayas developed a written language so complex that it still hasn't been completely translated.

Different Classes

Mayan society had five classes: a hereditary king, nobles, priests, farmers, and poor commoners and slaves captured in war. The slaves worked for their masters, and were often killed when their masters died so they could serve them in the afterlife. Most Mayas were farmers and their main crop was maize, or corn. They also grew avocados, pineapples, chilies, and cacao, which they made into a chocolate drink they mixed with water and hot chilies.

What is Beautiful?

The Mayas had a strong sense of beauty that was very different from today's standards. Noble families pressed their children's heads between boards so they would become flatter and longer. Parents dangled objects close to their children's faces so they would be cross-eyed. Mayan nobles, priests, and many

This pyramid ruin was once an important building in Tikal.

others filed their teeth to sharp points and inserted jade into the open spaces. They had many piercings and covered their bodies with tattoos. Men wore an *ex,* which is like a loincloth, and women wore sack-like cotton dresses. The nobles used finer fabrics for their clothing and decorated it with shells and beads.

Play Ball!

A ball game called *pitz* was an important part of Mayan culture. The Mayas invented a way to strengthen rubber to make the round heavy balls. (This was thousands of years before American Charles Goodyear figured it out in 1839.) They mixed sap from rubber trees with the juice of morning glory vines to make an elastic gum-like substance that could be molded into different shapes. This also made it bounce! The Spanish invaders took the pitz game over to Europe, where it became the basis for soccer and most of the other ball games we play today.

A Mysterious End

The Mayas began abandoning their cities and monuments around the year 905. No one knows why. Archeologists think it may have been because of disease, war with neighboring peoples, or because the Mayas could no longer farm their land. The Incas and Aztecs absorbed many of their customs and those cultures were still thriving when the Spanish arrived in the late 1500s.

女
Hana's Wedding

CHINA, TANG DYNASTY, 740

Morning

ana, there you are."

Hana turned as her brother, Shen, approached across the field.

"You are out early this morning."

"I wanted to see the sun rise. It is so beautiful here at the edge of the wheat field. Listen." She cupped a hand to her ear. "He sings such a happy song." She pointed to a yellow bird soaring across the brightening sky.

"You are feeling sentimental because this is your wedding day and you will leave us."

"So will you." She turned and looked up at her brother. "Are you happy to go to Chang'an? I would be afraid to live in such a big city. I hear it is made up of over a hundred neighborhoods, each larger than our own village. How will you not get lost?"

"I will learn my way," Shen said, smiling down at his sister. She wore a short-sleeved green silk tunic over a long brown skirt. Her thick black hair was piled on top of her head and held in place with a gold comb. As was the custom, she would marry the man her parents had chosen and go live in his house. *Will we see each other again?* Shen wondered. Chang'an was many miles away from their village and travel was difficult on China's rutted, muddy roads. Most people never left the village where they were born.

"Mother sent me to get you. You must be beautiful for your wedding."

Hana frowned. "And if I am not...?"

Shen took her hand. "You will be beautiful because you want to honor our parents' wishes; as I honor them by going to Chang'an to study for the government exam. It is difficult and will take many years of hard work. But if I pass, I will become a rich official and support our parents in their old age."

Hana sighed. "Growing up is not easy, is it?"

"No," said Shen. "But it is an adventure. Come." He took her hand. "Let us go home for our breakfast."

Their mother was waiting for them at the entrance to their house, a wood structure with four rooms and a kitchen built around a courtyard. Their father was a skilled craftsman who made pottery dishes that he sold in the village, and their home was comfortable and spacious. Hana and Shen followed their mother into the main room where their father, younger brother, and grandmother sat cross-legged around a low table.

"So you have come to join us?" Grandmother Qi gave them a stern look.

"We were listening to the birdsong," Hana said.

"You should be preparing for your wedding," snapped Grandmother.

As they knelt around the table to eat their meal of barley cakes, steamed fish, and tea, Hana thought about the day ahead. After breakfast she would go to her room to dress in her red silk robes. Then she would go to the house of Liang, her bridegroom, where she would meet him for the first time.

All Hana knew of Liang was that his father was a landowner with a bountiful farm. The astrologer her parents had consulted had checked the couple's birth charts to make sure they were compatible. Once the two families agreed to the marriage, Liang's parents sent betrothal gifts of clothing and jewelry. Among them was a coin engraved with the word *qui*, which meant "proposal." Hana's family had sent back a coin with the word *yun*, which meant they accepted the proposal. The families had then set about planning the wedding. And now the day was here and Hana would meet Liang and his mother, Ming Yu, the woman who would run Hana's life from this day forward; much as her grandmother ruled over her mother.

Hana held up a round bronze mirror and inspected her face. She had styled her eyebrows in the long and fine *emei* shape, applied a spot of rouge on each cheekbone, and painted the profile of a crimson flower on her mouth. Her hair was piled high and secured with gold pins. Her red silk skirt fell in soft folds to the tips of her finely crafted slippers.

Hana's mother turned her daughter around. "You are a beautiful bride."

"Mother, why must I leave my home to live in another house?"

"You cannot stay with your parents forever. You are thirteen years old—a woman now, and it is time for you to start your own family."

"But I will live under the rule of my husband's mother and must do as she says."

"That is the Chinese way." Her mother took Hana's face in her hands. "I came to your father's house and have had a happy life."

"Grandmother Qi is good to you."

"We have made our peace. Besides, do you think your father and I would choose an ogre for your mother-in-law? You seem more concerned about her than your bridegroom."

Hana blushed. "I pray you have chosen him wisely, as well."

"Now," said her mother, "I must go and dress."

As her mother left the room, Shen entered.

"May I come in?"

"Please, Brother, do."

"You cannot stay with your parents forever."

"You look lovely, my sister." He smiled. "Your bridegroom is a lucky man."

To his horror, Hana began to cry.

"What is this? You will ruin your makeup." He took a cloth from his pocket and dabbed at her eyes.

"Oh, Shen, I wish I were a man. Then I could go with you to Chang'an and study. I don't want to live in another woman's house and be her slave."

"I may be going to Chang'an, but I will still have a wife chosen for me and I, too, will have a mother-in-law." Shen set a finger under Hana's chin. He tilted her head and looked into her eyes. "You are a strong person with your own ideas. You will need to keep them to yourself and get along with whomever you must. I believe that you will make a good and happy life."

What does Shen know of being happy? Hana thought when her brother had left and she was alone in her room. Turning, she walked to the window and looked outside. A peasant in a conical straw hat was tilling the soil in the neighboring field. A pair of water buffalo pulled the plow while he walked behind, the reins resting in his outstretched hands. Suddenly she wanted to be out in the sunshine, breathing in the grain-scented air. Without pausing to think, Hana lifted her skirts and climbed through the window.

Hana crouched behind a tree. She heard her mother's voice, calling out her name. Shen, too, was looking for her. She had seen him walk to the field where they had talked that morning. Hana buried her face in her hands. What had prompted her to run away like a frightened puppy?

"May I sit here?"

Hana looked up to see a young man staring down at her. He wore cotton trousers and a loose blouse, both the color of wheat. His thick black hair was partly coiled into a topknot and the rest hung down his back in a braid. "Shhh." He pointed above their heads. Hana's gaze followed. A bright yellow bird perched on an upper branch.

"It sings a beautiful song," said the young man.

"Yes," Hana breathed. "I know it well, this bird."

He regarded her with laughing eyes. "And how, may I ask, have you made the acquaintance of such a free spirit as a songbird?"

"It sings to me every morning."

"And what does it sing?"

Hana closed her eyes. Above them the bird warbled its sweet tune. "It sings of my home; of my ancestors who watch over this home and keep it safe for my family."

The young man bent down and peered at her. "There are tears in your eyes as you tell me this. Why should that be?"

"Because today I must leave my family and go live with strangers."

The man's eyes widened. "Does this mean that your family is selling you?"

"Of course they are not selling me!" Hana said. Then, lowering her voice, "I am to be a bride."

"A bride." The man stood, hands on his hips, head tilted to one side. "Is this not every girl's dream, to marry and make a home?"

"It is not my dream. I would rather go to Chang'an with my brother to study for the government exams." When he remained silent, she continued. "My husband's house will not be *my* home. It will be that of my husband's mother and I will have to do as she says."

"And will not your husband have something to say about this?"

"Oh, he will listen to her, too. I cannot look to him for protection. I must obey this woman who will have a serpent's tongue and a heart of stone."

"And how do you know this? Perhaps this woman will be kind and gentle; a friend and not an enforcer."

"What do you know? You will not have to face such a fate."

"In that case, I wish you luck in your new life." He bowed and then lifted his eyes to the tree branches. "It seems our songbird has flown away."

"As I must, too." Hana rose to her feet. She smoothed her skirt, brushing bits of grass and leaves from the downy silk. "Thank you for your good wishes," she said, turning to address the man. But he was gone.

Afternoon

Where have you been?" Hana's mother flung open the door. "You look as if you were working in the fields."

Hana lowered her eyes. "I went to hear birdsong."

"Birdsong?" Her mother sighed. "Hana, you are not a child anymore. You are to be married and must act like a woman."

"I am still young. Perhaps it is too early for me to marry."

"Your bridegroom is waiting. Fix yourself up, for the ceremony is about to begin."

Hana peered out from the bridal sedan her groom's family had sent for her. It was red with gold trim and the four men holding the poles were dressed in red. Hana's silk robes and veil were also red, because that was the color of good luck. Her family walked outside the sedan while a band played and firecrackers popped. People crowded the road to watch as the noisy, joyous procession wended its way from the home of the bride to that of the groom. Hana shivered. In a few minutes she would leave her girlhood forever. She thought about her parents' instruction to be courteous and respectful and to obey her husband's commands. *What*, she wondered, *are my groom's parents telling him*? Tears sprang to her eyes. She was expected to cry tears of sorrow because she was leaving her parents' home, as well as tears of joy for her future life in her husband's home. Hana's tears were real.

The procession halted in front of her new family's home. The father, Wang, was a wealthy merchant and his house was large. The sedan

He stepped back and Hana's mouth fell open.

door opened and Hana stepped down. Her parents and grandmother, brothers, friends, and neighbors crowded around as she greeted Ming Yu, her new mother-in-law. Ming Yu was a stately woman with fine features in an oval face. Her black eyes swept over Hana, taking her measure from her elaborately coiled hairdo to her silk-slippered toes.

Hana willed her knees to stop shaking. She bowed to Ming Yu and then to Wang, a portly man in an elaborately embroidered robe.

"Welcome." He bowed. "May I present your bridegroom, Liang." He stepped back and Hana's mouth fell open.

"It is you," she breathed as she looked into the laughing eyes of the man she had met in the field.

"Yes." Liang bowed and, recovering from her shock, Hana returned his bow. Next the couple performed a series of ritual bows, which were called "bowing to Heaven and Earth" to ask approval of their marriage from the gods, ancestors, the couple's parents, grandparents, friends, and neighbors.

Following this ceremony, they were escorted into the bridal chamber, which had been decorated with furniture, pillows, scroll paintings, and draperies from the bride's dowry. Hana and her groom sat on the bed and the groom's elderly aunt fed them soup with small sweet dumplings. Next came the ceremony called the union of the wine cups. They were each handed a cup filled with rice wine. After they had sipped, the wine was poured into two more cups from which they drank again. The guests then showered them with nuts and candies that symbolized happiness.

When the formalities were over, the wedding party and guests retired to the courtyard for a grand feast.

Hana stood and looked at the man who was now her husband. "Did you know that I was your bride when you found me behind the tree?"

"I only dared to hope."

"Dared to hope?"

"Yes. That such a beautiful, strong-willed woman would be my bride."

"But men do not like their women to be strong willed. I have been taught that I must obey you. I cannot address you by name in public or touch you. I must bend to your will."

"That is in public," Liang smiled. "In private I want a wife who will be my partner and give me healthy children. Now come," he reached for her hand. "We must join our guests at the wedding feast."

Evening

The wedding celebrations lasted far into the night. At the banquet, Hana performed the ritual ceremony of presenting tea and wine to her parents, her in-laws and to Liang. Servants served dish after dish of succulent dumplings, steaming platters of chicken, pork, and fish, followed by dishes of nuts, melons, peaches, and plums. There was much music, laughter, and gaiety. Now it was time to bid her family farewell.

"You have made a beautiful and respectful bride." Her father smiled down at her. "May your marriage be blessed with peace, prosperity, and many sons."

Hana blushed. "Only sons?"

"Daughters, too. May your husband be blessed with a daughter such as mine."

Hana turned to her brother. "Tomorrow you leave for Chang'an. You will lead a different life in the city. Will I even know you when you return?"

"You will know me, for I will always be your brother." Shen bent down and kissed her cheek. "Have a good life, my sister. I will see you again."

As Hana watched her family leave, her spirits sank. Now she was truly alone in a house full of strangers. She turned and found her mother-in-law watching her. Was it her imagination or did Ming Yu look as tired as Hana felt?

"Do not be afraid of my mother," Liang said as he entered the bridal room. "She appears stern and wants us to fear her, but inside," he tapped his chest, "she is like that bird we saw this morning—full of song and light."

"Tomorrow you leave for Chang'an...will I even know you when you return?"

Hana doubted this but did not want to contradict her husband. "I will honor her and your father as I have honored my own parents."

Liang sat beside her. "Tomorrow I will take you to our family shrine to meet my ancestors so they can give approval to our marriage. You have nothing to fear."

"I am not afraid." Hana straightened her shoulders. Her feet hurt from standing up for hours greeting guests. Her head hurt from the noise of the bands and fireworks.

"Tell me, Hana, do you still wish to go to Chang'an to study with your brother?"

Hana thought for a moment. "I would like to be able to learn. It saddens me that girls are not allowed to go to school. But," she lowered her eyes, "now that I have met my husband, I am content to be a wife and mother."

"And do you still believe your mother-in-law has a serpent's tongue and a heart of stone?"

Hana's hands flew to her mouth. "Oh, I did say that, didn't I?"

"Yes," Liang laughed.

Hana looked around the room. It was in a strange house but filled with familiar things lovingly provided by her parents. She would make her life here. She looked at the man sitting beside her and suddenly her fear slipped from her shoulders like a discarded cloak. Her parents had chosen well. Liang was kind and gentle. He understood her longing for knowledge.

"Liang," she turned to face him, "tomorrow, after we meet your ancestors, I would like to return to the woods and find our yellow bird."

"To hear his song?"

"Yes, and to thank him for introducing me to my husband."

Liang threw back his head and laughed. "I will bring a cage and catch him so you can wake to his song every morning."

"No!" Hana looked at him in horror. "Do not take away his freedom. That will ruin his song."

"As marriage will ruin yours?"

"No." Hana shook her head. "I do not believe that this will happen."

Liang smiled. "Neither do I, my little bird. Neither do I." ∞

A Golden Age

THE TANG DYNASTY OF CHINA

The Tang Dynasty lasted from 618 to 907. It was a peaceful and successful era in which the Chinese people enjoyed their lives and customs. Under the Tang rulers, farmers were allowed to own their land, while in other times peasant farmers had to work for noblemen. Since the Tang rulers wanted to create a nation of farmers, they gave one *ch'ing* (about five acres) of land to each farmer. The farmers and their families worked hard, but they were happy and well fed.

City Life

Not everyone was a farmer. Some people were skilled craftsmen. Many people lived in cities, towns, and villages. The capital city, Chang'an, was home to over one million people. Those who wanted to become a high government official went there to study. To get a job in the government, they had to pass a very strict exam. Only men were allowed to take this exam. On examination day, the city was crowded with the horses and carriages of men who had studied for many years for the chance at a successful career.

Women at Home

Women were not allowed to go to school. They were raised to be wives and mothers and to take care of their homes. Families were very important. It was not unusual for children, parents, grandparents, aunts, uncles, and cousins to live together under the same roof. When a woman married, she would leave her parents' house and move in with her husband's family. She had no legal rights and could not inherit property. She had to obey her husband. She also had to obey her mother-in-law. In some cases, the new wife became her mother-in-law's servant.

This type of horse sculpture was popular during the Tang Dynasty.

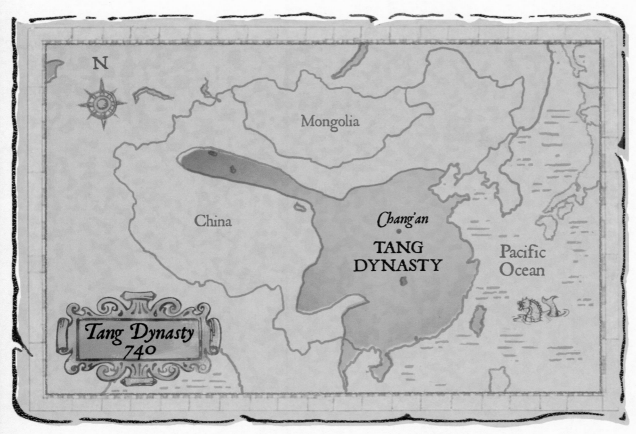

Tang Dynasty
740

Today, modern China is about twice as big as it was during the Tang Dynasty.

Shrine to Family

Ancestors have long been an important part of Chinese culture. During the Tang Dynasty, every home had an ancestral shrine. People believed their ancestors watched over and protected them. That is why a bride had to meet her new husband's ancestors to make the marriage official.

Time for Play

People's lives were not all work. They enjoyed music, dancing, and playing board games, such as backgammon. There were national holidays, too. Everyone celebrated the Emperor's birthday, which was a day of rest and fun for all Chinese.

Culture of Art

Chinese culture is rich with art. The people of the Tang Dynasty were skilled at painting, sculpture (especially statues of Buddha), and pottery, which they decorated with pictures of musicians, fantastical animals, and the signs of the zodiac. They also enjoyed entertainment. Bird concerts were very popular shows. Bird owners would gather and sip tea while their birds' songs filled the air. To those who listened, this heavenly music symbolized the voice of China.

A bronze censer. Incense was burned inside to give off a pleasant smell.

Jamal and the Doctor

BAGHDAD, ISLAMIC EMPIRE, 905

Morning

amal stood in the doorway of his house. Before the family stirred—before morning prayers and breakfast and the walk to his father's stall in the bazaar—he liked to watch the world awaken. The eastern sky was stained a light pink as dawn broke over Baghdad. A cock's crow tickled his ear.

"Good morning, Mr. Rooster," he smiled. "You, too, know that this day is special." For today, Ahmed the nomad would arrive with his camel loaded with the exotic goods that Jamal's father would sell in his stall.

Jamal rubbed his face. He had a cold and his nose and skin felt raw. His mother had given him herbal teas to ease his symptoms but his skin still itched. His tongue touched a blister inside his mouth and he winced.

Jamal went into the kitchen where his mother kept a bucket of water. Splashing his face calmed the itching. *I must have fleas in my sleeping mat*, he thought. *Tonight I will take it outside and beat it to chase them away.*

He turned as his mother came up behind him. "Good morning, my son," she said. "You are up early."

"I am to go with Father to meet Ahmed the nomad," Jamal said proudly. "I will help them unload the wares and set them up in the stall so Father can sell them." At the age of twelve, Jamal was the eldest of five children—three sons and two daughters—and was proud of his responsibilities.

"That is a very important job," said his mother. "You must have a good breakfast before you go." She leaned over. "Let me see your face." She frowned. "It is red."

Jamal touched his cheek. "It is nothing. Fleas." He grimaced.

At that moment his father entered the kitchen. "A good day to you."

"Fadi," his wife addressed him, "I do not think that Jamal is well. Perhaps he should not go to the bazaar today."

"I am fine." Jamal lifted his head and turned to his father. "My cold is better. Father, please let me come with you."

"You pamper the boy too much," Fadi said to his wife. He touched Jamal's forehead. "He *is* a bit warm."

"The day is hot. I am not sick."

"All right, then, you may come." His father lifted his head as the *muezzin*'s call to prayer drifted through the open window. "Come." He motioned for Jamal. "We will wash, and then say our morning prayers. After that, we can begin our day's business."

As they walked to the bazaar, Jamal thought how lucky he was to live in such a wondrous city. Baghdad was a bustling metropolis filled with palaces, libraries, schools, restaurants, and stores that sold goods from all over the world. When they reached the bazaar, it was bustling with activity. The air was fragrant with the smells of freshly baked bread, grilled meats, and savory spices. There were people everywhere, chattering and haggling over the price of a loaf of bread, a bolt of silk, or a precious emerald. They passed stalls overflowing with ivory from Africa, porcelain from China, and spices from India. As they walked, vendors called out greetings. "Good day, Fadi. Allah has blessed you with a healthy, strong son."

"The pox," he cried, pointing at Jamal. "The boy has the pox!"

Jamal beamed as people recognized his father. Fadi was respected as a great merchant. Jamal wanted to be just like him. Someday he would have his own stall, the biggest in Baghdad.

They reached Fadi's stall and stopped. A man in a white headband and long black robes was squatting on the ground, eating dates. He would pop one into his mouth, chew it carefully, and then turn his head and spit out the pit. At Jamal and his father's approach, he sprang to his feet and bowed. "*Wa alaikom assalam.*"

"*Wa alaikom assalam,*" Fadi returned the greeting. "It is good to see you, Ahmed. How was your trip from Damascus?"

"Hot and dusty." Ahmed wiped his forehead with his sleeve. "Ah, my friend, it takes courage and strength of will and body to cross the great desert, but by the grace of Allah, my caravan has arrived safe and sound. And," he added, "loaded down with merchandise for your pleasure." He turned to Jamal. "I see you have brought your son to help unload the camels."

"Yes," said Fadi. "This is my eldest boy, Jamal. He is learning to be a merchant."

"*Assalam Alaikom,*" said Jamal.

"*Wa alaikom assalam,*" replied Ahmed. He walked up to Jamal. Suddenly his smile disappeared. He stepped backwards so fast he stumbled and barely stopped himself from falling. "The pox," he cried, pointing at Jamal. "The boy has the pox!"

The bazaar became strangely silent as people turned to stare in horror. *Smallpox!* The dreaded word traveled up and down the street. Men ducked into their stalls. Women made the sign against the evil eye. Fadi grabbed Jamal and drew him aside. "Look at me," he commanded. He turned his son's face back and forth, studying the red blisters that had spread over his son's skin. "Fleas! You said you itched from fleas!"

"I thought it was fleas." Jamal's hands flew to his face. He felt bumps where earlier there had only been a rash. Was Ahmed right? Did he have the dreaded, contagious disease smallpox?

Jamal trembled. Was he going to die?

Afternoon

Jamal had never been in a *bimaristan* before. He sat on a stool in the waiting area, watching the bustling hospital activity as physicians and nurses treated patients who had come from all over Baghdad. The building was huge—like an enormous palace with many hallways and hundreds of rooms. The people filling the hospital came from all walks of life. Some wore the thinnest rags; others were dressed in fine silk clothing. There were women with jewels on every finger; others whose hands were worn and chapped. Babies cried in their mothers' arms. Children raced up and down the hall, playing games of tag to ease the boredom of waiting. Old men and women sat patiently, their eyes sunken in deeply wrinkled faces.

Jamal rested his chin in his hands and thought about all that had happened that morning. He had awakened full of excitement about Ahmed's visit and the chance to help his father in the stall. And now he was waiting to see a doctor who would tell him if he would live or die. How could this be? Then he remembered his symptoms—the runny nose, his aching head, and the telltale rash. *Maybe it is a cold*, he thought with a flash of hope. *Or maybe it is the pox.* His chin sank lower into his chest.

"Boy." A finger poked his chest. "Wake up."

"I'm not sleeping." Jamal turned and faced a thin man in a tattered cotton tunic. His skin was as dry as old leather and when he smiled, he revealed missing front teeth.

"I thought you would fall off your seat," the man chortled. "Are you waiting to see Dr. Al-Razi?"

"Who is Al-Razi?"

"He is the head of the Muqtadari Hospital, which is where you are now. Al-Razi is the greatest physician who ever lived." The man grinned and released a blast of foul breath. Jamal jerked backwards and his head bumped the wall.

The man peered at Jamal. "Do you know how Al-Razi chose this site to build his hospital?"

Jamal shook his head.

"He hung pieces of meat all over Baghdad and then checked to see which piece was the slowest to rot. He figured that would be the safest place for a hospital."

"That was very smart of him," said Jamal. He looked at the man. "How do you know all of this?"

"I've been here many times before." He laughed and Jamal tried not to gag.

"Have you come to have Al-Razi treat you for the pox?" asked the man. "I had it when I was a boy." He pointed to deep pit marks on his face. "It left me with these scars. But I lived. And now I am immune from the disease. Once you have it, you can never get it again."

"I'm glad you survived," said Jamal. *Maybe I will, too*, he thought. He looked around for his father. Where was he? Why didn't he come and rescue him from this man who stank of rotting teeth and made Jamal shake with fear?

As if his thoughts had conjured a genie, Jamal's father appeared. "Come." He motioned for Jamal to follow. "We must go to a different part of the hospital."

He followed his father down the hall. He noted how clean and neat everything was. Floors were freshly scrubbed, the walls were free of dust and grime, and the doctors and nurses were dressed in immaculate tunics.

They turned a corner and a nurse showed them into a small room.

"I'm sorry, Father," Jamal said when they were settled on a bench. "Sorry that I took you away from the bazaar on the day that Ahmed arrived with the caravan."

"Ahmed will wait." His father placed a hand on Jamal's knee. "Your health is more important."

Jamal sighed. He closed his eyes and drifted off to sleep. A fly landing on his nose woke him. The air was thick with Baghdad's suffocating noon heat. He looked to his right. His father's eyes were closed. When he breathed, soft snores fluttered from his mouth.

Jamal stood and stretched. He stepped into the hallway and almost bumped into a young girl. Remembering that his disease might be contagious, he stepped back. The girl looked up at him and smiled. Jamal looked at the girl. Her clothes were ragged and her face was dirty and covered in scabs. "Hello," he said. "My name is Jamal. What is yours?"

"Leyla." She smiled shyly.

Jamal pointed to her face. "The pox?" he asked.

The girl shrugged. She lowered her eyes.

"Leyla, come here." A woman took the girl's arm. She, too, was dressed in pale frayed cotton and her head was covered with a scarf that must once have been white but was now a dingy gray. She looked at Jamal out of the same big dark eyes as the girl. "It is our turn to see Dr. Al-Razi," she said. "We must not keep the great doctor waiting."

Jamal watched them enter an examining room. He walked back to the bench and sat next to his father, who was now awake. "Father, those people look so poor. How will they pay the doctor?"

"They will not need to pay. Anyone can come here—rich or poor. The hospital is free for all who need help."

Jamal digested this fact. "I think Dr. Al-Razi is a great man for building such a hospital."

"Yes," said his father. "And it is thanks to the Caliph Al-Muqtader that he had the funds to do this. We are lucky to have a ruler who cares so much for his people." He looked up as a nurse beckoned them. "Come, it is our turn to see the doctor."

Jamal sat on a table as Dr. Al-Razi examined his face. His heart pounded. Would the doctor pronounce him ill with smallpox? Was he going to be scarred for life, like the old man in the hallway? Or worse, would he die like so many others stricken with the dreaded disease? He looked past the doctor's head at his father, whose face showed the same fear that he himself felt.

Dr. Al-Razi began by touching Jamal's forehead to see if he had a temperature. Next he checked his pulse. He then asked the boy a series of questions. When did he first notice the rash? Did his head hurt? Was any other part of his body sore? He looked in Jamal's eyes and inside his mouth, and then he smiled. "You are lucky, young man. What you have is a case of the measles. Measles is a much less serious disease than smallpox. You will need to spend a few days resting and then you will be as good as new." He turned to Fadi. "Measles can hurt the eyes. Keep the boy in a darkened room."

Jamal let out his breath. Measles! He was not going to be disfigured. He was not going to die.

"How do you tell the difference between the two diseases?" Jamal's father asked.

The doctor leaned against the wall and folded his arms. "Until recently, people thought that measles and smallpox were the same disease. I have spent a great deal of time studying the symptoms and was able to prove that they are, indeed, two separate ailments. In both, eruptions appear on the skin; however, smallpox eruptions appear together in groups and dig down into the skin. Measles spread across the skin as a rash that does not penetrate the skin. Your son has blisters in his mouth, which is a symptom of measles, not smallpox. Both diseases come with fever and body aches, but the smallpox symptoms are more severe."

Jamal looked at the doctor with respect. "Did you discover all of this by yourself?

Dr. Al-Razi laughed. "I have spent many years studying patients and their symptoms. Now that we can distinguish smallpox from measles, we can treat patients sooner. There is no cure for the pox," he sighed, "but we treat the patients' wounds, lower their fevers, and help them regain strength."

"Did that girl Leyla have smallpox?" asked Jamal.

"No." The doctor frowned. "Poverty causes many illnesses."

"I think you are wonderful for treating everyone who comes here for free," Jamal blurted out.

"In Islam we believe that all of Allah's children deserve to be cared for when they are sick. Our Prophet Mohammed said 'Make use of medical treatment, for Allah has not made a disease without appointing a remedy for it, with the exception of one disease, namely old age.'" The doctor winked. "Even this great hospital cannot cure that ailment, I'm afraid." He put his hand on Jamal's shoulder. "Remember the Prophet's words, young man, and always take care of those in need."

Evening

easles." Jamal's mother sighed with relief. "You must stay in your bed until the rash is gone," she told Jamal.

"But I want to help father in the bazaar."

"Next time." His father looked at him sternly. "You are lucky to have measles, but it is also a serious disease. You can pass it to others. You must stay in your room, away from light. Ahmed will return in two months' time. You may help me then."

Jamal lay on his sleeping mat. It felt good to be in a darkened room. The light hurt his eyes. He had learned that, in severe cases, measles could even cause blindness. His mother had brought him broth. After he ate, she had bathed his skin with cloths soaked in cool water and applied a salve to soothe the itching. Now he was supposed to sleep. It was strange to be alone. Normally his brothers and sisters would be on their sleeping mats next to him but, because measles was contagious, they had moved to the front room.

He closed his eyes but couldn't sleep. So much had happened today. He had gone to the bazaar with his father, met Ahmed the nomad, been whisked to the bimaristan, and met the great doctor Al-Razi. Rising to his feet, he walked to the window. A soft breeze brushed his skin. It reminded him of the doctor's gentle touch as he examined the eruptions on Jamal's face.

Jamal leaned on the windowsill and rested his chin in his hands. Dr. Al-Razi was a great man because he treated everyone the same. People came to his hospital with their ailments and received medical care without charge. On the way home, Jamal's father talked of Al-Razi's reputation as a man of charity. He said that the doctor earned large amounts of money, but gave most of it away. Dr. Al-Razi had written over one hundred books about medicine to teach others to use the treatments he had discovered.

I want to be a doctor just like him, Jamal thought, then fought back a sharp pang of guilt. How could he be a doctor? He was going to be a merchant, like his father. He would have the biggest stall in the bazaar. Camel caravans would stretch across the desert, carrying goods from all over the world for him to sell. After all, that was important work too—selling people the things they need to live comfortable lives. A voice tickled his ear. *But how can they enjoy silks and wonderful foods if they are not healthy?*

Jamal turned his head, but the room was empty. It was his own heart speaking. He walked back to his mat and was about to lie down when his father entered.

"So, my son, how are you feeling?"

"Much better, Father."

"You had quite an experience today." His father motioned for Jamal to sit and then sank cross-legged on the floor beside him. "What did you think of the bimaristan?"

"I think it is a miraculous place."

"Miraculous? And what miracles did you see performed?"

"I saw a building the size of a palace where everyone can get free care. I saw beggars treated like noblemen. And," Jamal paused and took a deep breath, "I discovered what I want to do when I am grown."

"And that is?"

"Please do not be angry at me, Father. But I think I will be a doctor."

"And why do you think I would be angry, my son?"

"You will be disappointed in me. Until today I wanted to be a merchant like you."

"And now you wish to heal people."

"Yes, Father. I want to learn what makes people sick and find ways to cure them."

His father smiled. "That is a noble ambition, Jamal. I am proud of you. Now, you must sleep, so you will get well. Until you are a great doctor, you can still help me in the bazaar. You will be amazed to see the beautiful silks that Ahmed has brought from China. And from India, jewels that dazzle the eye."

After his father left, Jamal lay on his mat, arms folded behind his head. He closed his eyes and smiled. His face itched, his eyes burned, and his head still ached. But his heart was happy. Someday he would study with Dr. Al-Razi and his staff at the bimaristan and learn to help others, just as the doctor had helped him. ∞

The Story of Dr. Al-Razi
THE ISLAMIC EMPIRE

The holy book of Islam is called the Koran.

The *bimaristan* of Baghdad was one of the finest hospitals ever built. Its name means "asylum of the sick." It was founded by the great Islamic doctor Muhammad ibn Zakariya Al-Razi, or Rhazes. Dr. Al-Razi was born in 865 in the city of Rayy, near Tehran, in what is now the country of Iran. In 901, he went to Baghdad, in what is now Iraq. This city was one of the most important centers of knowledge in the world.

Care for All

At this time, scholars of all kinds gathered in Baghdad, but especially those who studied medicine. Baghdad's bimaristan treated all people, whatever their sickness, whether they were male or female, young or old, rich or poor. The idea for the hospital came from Islamic culture, in which it was important to care for the sick and the poor.

Medical Masters

Islamic scholars learned from Greek, Roman, Persian, Syrian, Indian, and Byzantine sources. They added their own observations and many wrote medical texts. Dr. Al-Razi was the most respected of these scholars. He accomplished many great things. He was an excellent diagnostician, which is someone who looks at a person's physical problems. He asked his patients about every detail of their disease and then observed them. He believed that taking a complete medical history was the first step in treating a patient.

Dr. Al-Razi treated many young, sick children in Baghdad.

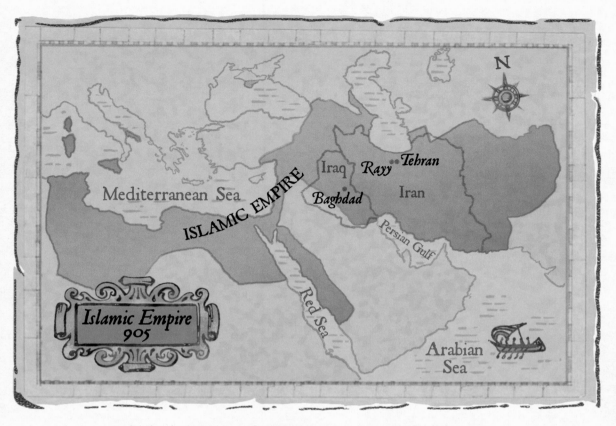

N

Mediterranean Sea

ISLAMIC EMPIRE

Iraq

Rayy • *Tehran*

Baghdad • Iran

Persian Gulf

Red Sea

Arabian Sea

Islamic Empire 905

Baghdad and Tehran are now found in the modern-day countries of Iraq and Iran.

A Brilliant Mind

Dr. Al-Razi achieved many firsts. He was the first doctor to recognize that measles and smallpox are two different diseases. He was the first to test new drugs on animals, such as monkeys. He invented a suture—which is like a strong thread—made from cat gut to stitch up wounds. He was also the first doctor to distinguish whether a hemorrhage—bleeding inside the body—is from a vein or an artery. He described how to remove cataracts from the eye. One of his most important discoveries was that a fever is a symptom, or a sign, of a disease, not the disease itself.

Not Just a Doctor

Dr. Al-Razi was a polymath—a person who is an expert in several different fields. He wrote many books that discuss subjects such as chemistry, religion, and philosophy. But he is mainly remembered as one of the greatest doctors and medical thinkers of the medieval world. His most well-known book is *The Encompassing Book on Medicine,* which is a collection of all the medical knowledge of his day. He made a great deal of money in his life but gave most of it away to charity. Dr. Al-Razi returned to Rayy in 907 and lived there until he died in 925.

A Sad Departure

Morning

I ngrid! Ingrid! Where are you?"

I am hiding behind a tree. My mother is looking for me and I do not want to be found. At least not right now. Not until I speak to Shawnadithit. We have been friends almost since the day I arrived in Vinland and I do not want to leave without saying goodbye. Just because the adults from my settlement fought with the adults from Shawnadithit's tribe does not mean that she and I must part as enemies.

"Ingrid! Come back here this minute!"

My mother's voice is getting closer. I rose before dawn to escape my parents' attention. How many times have I traveled this same route through the woods to the natives' camp? How many times have I come to pick berries or the wild grapes that inspired my people to call this place Vinland? In the four years since we came here from Greenland, I have grown to love the land and the natives, or Beothuk, who inhabit it. Our people call them *Skraelings*—an insulting term that I will not use. For four years, our two peoples have gotten along. Now, after a disastrous battle, the Beothuk are forcing us to leave.

My family was part of a small group that sailed here from Greenland in 998, hoping to start a settlement in a fertile new land. We were attracted by the forests and vegetation and the plentiful animals and fish. When the Viking explorer Erik the Red discovered Greenland in 982, he gave it a name that he hoped would attract settlers. But the name misrepresented the cold, barren land to which my family will now return.

"Ingrid, over here."

I hear Shawnadithit's soft, whispered voice. She, too, is creeping through the forest

to our meeting place. As I rush to meet her, I stumble over a root. I reach for a trunk to steady myself as Shawnadithit appears.

"Still learning the ways of the forest," my friend laughs as she steps from behind a tree.

"There are no forests in Greenland," I reply sadly.

We regard each other. We are both twelve years old, but very different. I have fair skin, blue eyes, and fiery red hair that I wear in two long braids. Shawnadithit has black eyes and thick, shiny black hair that tumbles down her back. Her dark skin is covered with red ocher paint in the manner of her people.

"Why do your people use that paint?" I asked her the first time we met.

"It protects us from insects. And it is pretty," she replied.

We did not, at that time, speak the same language. We communicated by a sign language we developed between ourselves. Over the past four years, we taught each other many words by pointing to objects and repeating their names. I visited Shawnadithit's camp and met her mother and father and entered the tribe's homes, called *mamteeks*. These cone-shaped wooden houses, covered in birch bark, are very different from the long wooden houses built by my people, the Vikings. The Beothuk gather birds' eggs and plants along the coast. They catch fish with spears and hunt seals and caribou. Shawnadithit showed me all this and I was proud to learn her culture and to speak the Beothuk tongue. Most of my people did not take the trouble to do this, although some, including my brother, followed my lead.

I greet Shawnadithit cautiously and follow her through the dense underbrush to a clearing near a narrow stream. This is our special meeting place. In summer, we picked wild raspberries here and ate them until our mouths were stained as red as Shawnadithit's body paint. Now, in late April, the bushes are beginning to sprout tender green leaves. I won't be here for the berry season. The thought makes me sad.

Shawnadithit sits on the ground cross-legged and I join her. It is hard for me, with my long wool skirt and leather-booted feet, to sit comfortably in that position. She often teases me about my clothes. She asks why I would wear such cumbersome garments when I could dress in the comfortable style of the Beothuk. Their women wear skirts of animal skins that come to their knees and a wrap-around mantle on their upper bodies. In the winter, they wear leather mittens and soft leather moccasins.

I sit and fold my skirt over my legs. The ground is damp but I don't care if I get mud on my clothes. We look at each other awkwardly. Two days earlier, Shawnadithit's people attacked our settlement. My father suffered a serious injury when an arrow pierced his shoulder. Our people fought back and several Beothuk were wounded. One was killed.

"Why has this happened?" I look into Shawnadithit's dark, terror-filled eyes.

"Your people tried to kill us," she replies. "You gave us poison to drink."

"We gave you milk. Milk is good."

"It made us sick. It is poison, like one of these." Shawnadithit plucks a mushroom and holds it out to me. "This plant kills. Your drink kills, too."

"No! Milk does not kill. Babies drink milk."

"Mother's milk is good. Your milk from cows is poison."

"No one died from it." I sigh. How can I make Shawnadithit understand that my people meant no harm? When we arrived, the Beothuk visited our settlement to trade. They brought animal skins and nuts and berries. In return they wanted red cloth. The trading went well until we recently ran out of cloth. So we offered them cow's milk instead. At first the Beothuk were intrigued by this strange new drink. But when many became ill, the troubles started.

"Please believe me," I plead. "We meant no harm."

Shawnadithit reaches for my hand. "We," she points at me and then at herself, "are still friends."

"Get away from her!"

I jump to my feet at my brother's voice. "Thor, what are you doing here?"

"Mother sent me to look for you." He glares at Shawnadithit. "How can you sit here talking to that Skraeling while our father lies close to death from their arrows?"

"Do not use that word," I shout. "And father's shoulder wound will heal."

Thor grabs my arm. "It has become infected. He is burning with fever. Come. Unless you want to remain here after your people have left this cursed place!"

With an apologetic look at Shawnadithit, I follow my brother home.

> "Your people tried to kill us. You gave us poison to drink."

Afternoon

 t the settlement, people are busy packing. Into wooden crates go metal axes, hammers, and metal bone cutters. I watch as our neighbor, Hilde, takes apart the loom she uses to weave the wool cloth that is sewn into clothing for the encampment's men, women, and children.

Our people have only been on Vinland for four years and our settlement is quite sparse. It consists of several longhouses, a corral for the cows, and a sauna, or bath house, for our weekly Saturday baths. The longhouses are rectangular buildings made of wood. Each is built around a hearth, a fireplace used to cook and keep the interior warm.

"Where have you been?" My mother races up to me. Her usually pale skin is flushed with anger and her eyes are puffy. "I thought those savages had killed you."

"They are not savages."

"And what else would you call people who attack for no reason?"

"They had a reason. They thought we were poisoning them."

"Poison! We gave them cloth and milk and they repaid us with arrows."

"Now, Menja, it was a terrible mistake." Sven, the settlement's doctor, puts a hand on mother's shoulder. "The poor creatures cannot tolerate the food that we take for granted."

"And so they come storming out of the woods, with bows and arrows and stone axes? Poor creatures indeed! Now I must tend to my husband who is fighting for his life. Ingrid, come with me." She pulls me into the longhouse.

It takes a moment for my eyes to adjust to the darkness. When they do, I see my father lying still as a log on a wooden platform on the far side of the room. Only his face, pale as snow, and his bright red beard are visible above layers of fur robes and feather quilts. I step forward and cough. A fire is burning in the hearth. The smoke curls up through the smoke hole in the wood-beamed ceiling. Not all of it makes it out and the house is filled with a haze that makes my nose itch and my eyes water.

I turn to my mother. "Is Papa…?"

"No. Papa is not dead. Yet!" She crosses the room and kneels by my father's side. She places a hand on his forehead. She touches his cheek and then his forehead again and jumps to her feet. "Ingrid, get the doctor. Now!"

I run from the house. I find the doctor and tug at his sleeve. "Mama wants you."

The doctor turns and races into the house. I start to follow him but Thor holds me back. "How could you meet with that girl? I do not understand you, Ingrid."

I turn from my brother. All around me, people are preparing to leave. Two ships sit in the harbor, waiting to receive the boxes of clothing and equipment piled on the shore. With a sinking heart I realize that my family is truly returning to Greenland. But even worse, the men are arming themselves for a last fight with the Beothuk.

I must warn Shawnadithit. In spite of what Thor says, she is my friend. I have to let her know that her people are in danger.

As I dash along the river I feel like I am being torn in half. I pray that my father will not die and at the same time I understand why the Beothuk attacked. They thought they were being poisoned. Then our people killed one of their men. Maybe my father had even swung the fatal axe. I think of the day we arrived in Vinland. How strange we must have appeared in our big boats with the huge sails, and our tall men with their ice blue eyes and fiery red beards. Shawnadithit's people had gathered to greet us. I noticed Shawnadithit hiding behind her mother. I watched as her father, the tribe's chief, stepped forward. *How brave he is*, I thought, as I saw him greet our men with a sign of peace. And to my delight, my people responded. No blows were exchanged. The natives returned to their camp while we set up ours. Several days later, when I was in the forest searching for berries, I came upon Shawnadithit. The native girl showed me which fruit could be eaten and which could not. We learned to trust each other.

I stop suddenly. At the river's edge, I see six Beothuk men poised with their spears and bows and arrows. I dart behind a tree so they won't see me. Are they preparing for another attack on the settlement? I have come to warn them of my people's attack, but now it seems that both sides are ready for war. I see Shawnadithit emerge from the woods. She runs up to a tall man, whom I recognize as her brother, and grabs his arm.

> "Please, do not attack. Let the strangers leave in peace."

"Please, do not attack," Shawnadithit begs. "Let the strangers leave in peace."

Her brother pushes her away and continues to test his bow. The other men gather around. They shout at Shawnadithit and one shoves her so hard she stumbles and falls to the ground. Struggling to her feet, she continues to plead, but the men ignore her.

"You attacked them first," Shawnadithit cries.

"They poisoned us." Her brother snarls. "This is not a place for a girl. Go home! I will deal with you when we return."

"*If* you return!" she calls out as the men move away. Distressed, Shawnadithit turns and runs into the woods. I call out to her, but she doesn't hear. So I follow.

Branches tear at my clothes. I trip over tree roots and, more than once, almost fall. I am desperate to keep her in my vision but she moves like a deer through the forest and I can't keep up. Panting for breath, I stop walking and lean against a tree. I close my eyes and visualize the scene that is now taking place. The men of Shawnadithit's tribe are moving stealthily forward, their bows and arrows poised for attack. On the shore, the Viking men, too, are arming for battle even as the women are preparing to leave. I recall how fascinated Shawnadithit was with the loom on which my mother weaves cloth and the metal needles she uses to sew the cloth into garments. Mother promised to teach Shawnadithit to use them. Now she will never learn. I sigh.

Suddenly, I jump as a loud crash brings my attention back to the present. Has the battle started? I whirl around. Before me is the biggest, angriest bear I have ever seen.

"Do not move," a familiar voice hisses in my ear.

"Is that you, Shawnadithit?" I whisper.

"I said, 'DO NOT MOVE!'"

The bear lumbers toward us. It sniffs, then stops and sniffs again. Then it lurches forward. I feel the air move as the giant animal lunges toward me, its terrible claws reaching for my face.

Thwack! An arrow whizzes above my head.

The bear stops in mid-strike.

Thwack! A second arrow strikes. *Thump!* The bear falls to the ground.

I look up into the angry face of Shawnadithit's brother.

"What are you doing here?" he asks.

"I…I came to warn you that our men…"

"And I came to warn you about our men…" Shawnadithit turns to me.

At that moment, a group of Vikings led by Thor, crashes through the underbrush. Thor holds up his hand and the men halt. He looks from me to the dead bear and then to the Beothuk.

"You saved them," said Thor in a mixture of our language and theirs.

"Yes. Now take your sister and leave us in peace."

"No." I stamp my foot. "We should all go to the settlement together and make peace." Suddenly I remember the still-as-death figure on the pallet in the longhouse and my mother's frantic call for the doctor. "Thor, is Father…?"

"His fever has broken. He will live." Thor turns to the others. "Your arrow wounded but did not kill."

"Unlike your spears," scowled a Beothuk.

I walk up to Shawnadithit. "I came to warn you of the attack, but also to give you this." I reach into my pocket, pull out a needle, and place it in Shawnadithit's palm.

She curls her fingers over it. "I will think of you when I use it."

We embrace. Then Shawnadithit follows her brother and his men to the humpbacked canoes, bobbing in the river, for the trip to her village. I walk with Thor and the other Viking men to the Vinland settlement.

Evening

 enter the longhouse. What will I find?

My father is sitting upright on his pallet. My mother sits on a low stool beside him, spooning broth into his mouth. He gives me a weak smile.

"Father, you are alive." I walk over and sit beside him.

"It seems the natives did not finish me."

"Shawnadithit says her people believe we poisoned them."

Father sighs. "For a time, I thought we would live here in peace and make a home. Now it is impossible."

"But if it is a mistake, can we not correct it, Father?"

"It is better to leave now and return to Greenland, where we belong."

"Ingrid, do not tire your father with this chatter." My mother turns to him. "Harald, finish this broth. It will give you strength."

I leave the longhouse and walk to the enclosure where the cattle are housed. Opening the gate, I step inside. A newborn calf nuzzles against my leg.

"Hello, Astrid." I cup the calf's face in my hands. The calf's mother ambles over and moos loudly. "Dalla, how could your milk cause so much trouble?"

The cow moos in reply and I laugh.

"Ingrid!"

I turn as my brother approaches.

"Yes, Thor?"

"Stay here. No more wandering into the woods."

"No, Thor. I have done what I needed to do."

"And what was that?"

"Prevent more fighting between our people and the Beothuk."

He grunts. I leave him and walk to the shore. Night is falling and the large ships, their sails lowered, rest at anchor in the bay. Tomorrow they will be loaded with the last of the crates, the cattle and, finally, our people. Then we will leave Vinland forever. I sit on a large flat-topped rock, look across the water, and see the spout of a whale. Seagulls circle overhead, their screeches rising above the crash of the waves. I think of Greenland, the land where I was born. It is barren, with little vegetation, but at least it is on the sea. There will be whales and gulls, but I will miss Vinland's trees and the birds that nest in their branches. I will miss bushes thick with berries and streams dancing with fish. But most of all, I will miss Shawnadithit.

I rise and walk up the beach. Before entering the longhouse, I turn to look at the forest. Is it my imagination or do I see a head with shiny dark hair and two black eyes peering out at me from behind a tree? I strain to see through the gathering dusk, but shadows gather and the image is gone. Was it really Shawnadithit or only my imagination conjuring one last look at my friend?

I turn from the forest and enter the longhouse to spend my last night in Vinland. ∞

A Viking Saga

THE VINLAND SETTLEMENT

The history of Vinland, the Viking settlement in North America, is based on two Norse sagas, or stories. For centuries, there was no physical evidence that the Norse people had actually been in North America. But in the 1960s, archeologists found artifacts of a Viking settlement from around 998 at L'Anse aux Meadows, in what is now the northwestern tip of Newfoundland, Canada.

Great Explorers

The Viking people were from Denmark and Norway. They first settled in Iceland around the year 800. By 975, it was getting crowded. So in 982, the Viking explorer Erik the Red went looking for new lands. He discovered Greenland. Even though it didn't have much trees or grass, he called it Greenland to attract people to live there.

Life in Greenland

In 985, several hundred Vikings left Iceland to colonize Greenland. Since the land was not suited for farming crops, the settlers raised sheep and goats. Eventually, they cut down so many trees that the land became unusable. According to the sagas, in 986 an Icelandic merchant ship owner named Bjarni Herjulfsson was caught in a terrible storm out at sea. When the storm ended, he saw land that was thickly forested. He knew this wasn't Greenland. When he returned home, he told people of his discovery. Leif Erickson, the son of Erik the Red, was curious. He retraced Herjulfsson's voyage and eventually reached a land of trees, meadows, and rivers full of salmon. He called this place Vinland.

The settlement at L'Anse aux Meadows has been restored to look as it did one thousand years ago.

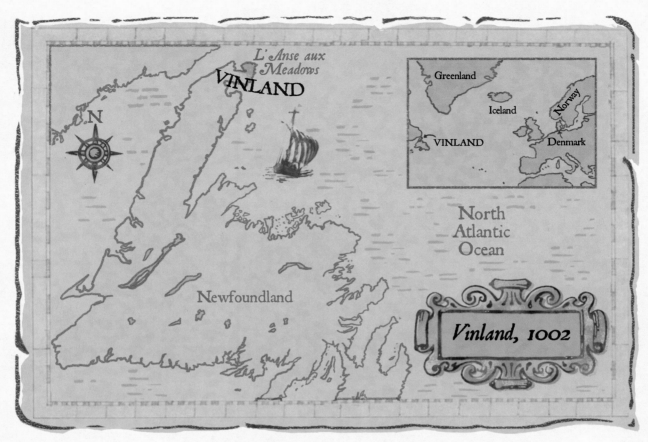

Viking explorers from Denmark and Norway had to cross the Atlantic Ocean to reach Iceland, Greenland, and Vinland.

Off to Vinland

According to the sagas, plenty of grapes, timber, and wheat grew in Vinland. Leif Erickson encouraged others to settle there—Thorfinn Karsefni, a trader from Iceland, led a group of settlers who brought livestock. Historians think these people stayed in Vinland for about four years. It's believed that fighting between the settlers and natives caused the Vikings to leave. One theory is that when the Vikings traded with the natives and gave them milk, the natives couldn't digest it. The natives thought they were being poisoned and attacked the settlers.

Strange Departure

To this day, no one knows exactly where Vinland was or why it was abandoned. The discovery of L'Anse aux Meadows proves that the Vikings were in Newfoundland, but historians and archeologists are not sure whether it was just a camp for repairing Viking ships or a farming settlement as the sagas say it was. Perhaps someday another discovery will reveal Vinland's true location and purpose.

The forests of Vinland were a welcome sight to Vikings from Greenland, where few trees grew.

Richard's Dilemma

England, 1197

Morning

Richard hurried through the corridor, buttoning his tunic as he ran. He shivered. The morning was cold and damp and he was late for mass. *You are no longer a page*, he reminded himself. *You are a squire.* He brushed a lock of black hair from his eyes. *Squire!* It was his final step to becoming a knight. Of course knighthood was still many years and much hard work away. But at twelve years of age, his journey had begun. Or had it?

"Richard," his friend Henry, who was also a squire, hissed as Richard slipped into the chapel. "You are late. Lord Geoffrey does not like tardiness."

Richard sank to his knees. He had lain awake much of the night, gripped with fear. A messenger had arrived yesterday with news from home. His eldest brother, George—who was the head of the family since their father's recent death—had sent word that there was no longer money for Richard's knighthood training. He would have to return home.

Richard looked around the chapel. It was two stories high. Lord Geoffery's family sat in a rear balcony while everyone else sat in front. The priest stood on a raised platform behind a table on which was placed a tall wooden cross. As the priest chanted the mass, Richard sniffed the familiar scent of incense and closed his eyes. He loved the ritual of this morning service. It gave him a sense of peace.

After the service, Richard and Henry returned to their quarters for a small breakfast of bread and ale. Today, the main meal of the day would be a special one. It would be served in the castle's great hall at mid-morning. After breakfast, Richard and Henry left the keep—the section of the castle where Lord Geoffrey's family and servants lived—

crossed the courtyard, and entered the stables. As a squire, Richard was responsible for maintaining the equipment of Sir Kenneth, the knight who was, in turn, training him for battle. That meant keeping Sir Kenneth's armor and weapons clean and in good condition. It also meant grooming Lion Heart, Sir Kenneth's horse.

"Good morning, Sir Richard."

"I am not *Sir* Richard. I'm only a squire." Richard greeted Michael, the castle's newest page. He tousled the boy's blond hair. The seven-year-old page had come to the castle a fortnight ago. He came from a noble family in the north of England, near the shire where Richard's family lived. Michael reminded Richard of himself when he had arrived five years earlier. He had been terrified. Although Lord Geoffrey and Richard's father were childhood friends, Richard had only met the lord once before coming to live in his castle. At first he missed his parents, his three brothers, and younger sister. But as he adjusted to castle life, the fear and loneliness was replaced by a sense of excitement and pride. He would try to help Michael as Sir Kenneth, who was then a squire, had helped him.

Norman, the stableman, tapped him on the shoulder, breaking his thoughts. "It's time for you and the page here to muck out the stables." He handed each boy a shovel. "And when you're done, Sir Kenneth wants Lion Heart groomed."

> ## "I am not *Sir* Richard. I'm only a squire."

Richard was happy to work keeping Sir Kenneth's armor shiny. And caring for the knight's horse made him feel useful and important. Lion Heart whinnied as they approached. Richard reached up to rub the horse's nose. "He is the fastest horse in the castle," he bragged to Michael. "Do you know why Sir Kenneth named him Lion Heart? Because he was sired by the horse that Sir Kenneth's father rode when he went to fight in the Holy Land with King Richard the Lionheart. I was named after the king, as well."

At that moment, a tall man in a dark green tunic, black leggings, and soft leather boots entered the stable. A green cap sat jauntily on top of his shoulder-length brown hair. "Sir Kenneth." Richard bowed.

"Have you checked my armor?" Sir Kenneth gave Richard a stern look. "It must be in perfect condition. No spots of rust or squeaky hinges."

"You will have the best armor in the tournament."

"Good." The knight patted Richard's shoulder and then looked at Michael. "And who is this young man?

"Michael. He is the new page."

"Welcome, Michael." Sir Kenneth smiled at the boy. "I wish you Godspeed in your new post." He stroked his horse. "We are going to win today, aren't we Lion Heart?"

Lion Heart whinnied and pawed the ground.

Richard's heart was heavy as he watched Sir Kenneth walk away. *I will see that you are the most prepared knight in the joust,* he thought, as he remembered the letter. *If it is to be my last time, it will be my best.*

The mid-morning meal was the highlight of the castle's day. It was served in the great hall and when there were guests—as there were on this day—it could last for two hours. There was a strict set of rules for behavior at mealtimes. Richard relayed these to Michael as they walked across the courtyard on their way to the castle.

"Always wash your hands before and after you eat. Don't slurp your soup. Don't blow your nose with your fingers and don't belch or spit at the table. Don't wipe your mouth on the tablecloth and never pass gas at the table. Just watch me and do as I do."

They passed the bakehouse, which was located away from the keep to lessen the danger of fire from the wood ovens. When they reached the castle, they climbed a set of winding stone steps to the entrance. It was on the second floor to make it difficult for invaders to enter.

They entered the great hall, which was the center of activity. It was a grand room with a high wood-beamed ceiling. The walls were hung with brilliantly colored rugs and tapestries, many brought by Lord Geoffrey's father when he returned from far-away Syria after the holy wars.

Lord Geoffrey and his wife, Lady Anne, were seated on high-backed chairs at a long table on a dais, a raised platform at the front of the hall. Lord Geoffrey wore a dark red robe trimmed with black velvet. His graying hair was topped by a black cap. Lady Anne's dress was a light blue silk with gold trim and a matching veil over her blond hair, which was pulled into a knot at the back of her head. Only those on the dais had chairs. Everyone else sat on benches placed before low trestle tables that would be dismantled and stored after the meal. People were seated in order of importance, with the most powerful closest to the dais. Richard, Michael, and Henry were at the back of the room. They shared a plate and a cup. Each had his own spoon.

Once everyone was seated, waiters brought jugs of water to each table so the diners could wash their hands. The nobles were served first. The boys waited and talked quietly.

"Who are the guests?" Richard asked.

"The man on Lord Geoffrey's left is Lord Williams," said Henry. "He is a powerful noble who wants to form an alliance with Lord Geoffrey. The man on Lady Anne's right is Sir Robert. He is Sir Kenneth's opponent in the joust."

Richard looked at his friend with respect. "How do you know all of this?"

Henry grinned and pointed to his eyes and then his ears. "I watch. And listen."

"He listens at keyholes," laughed a red-haired girl seated beside him. She tossed her head and a long curl escaped the lacy veil pinned to the back of her hair.

"And Catherine listens to her mistress's conversations!" Henry turned to her. "Why are you here? Aren't you supposed to sit with the other ladies-in-waiting?"

"I wanted to be near you." Catherine smiled coyly.

Richard watched them jealously. Although he and Henry were friends, there was much competition between them. Richard was a better archer, but Henry was quicker with a lance. And Henry was skillfully mastering the knightly art of chivalry toward girls—an art that the shyer Richard found difficult.

A waiter appeared with a tray of roasted venison and salted fish. Richard was ravenous. He dug into the food, eating with his fingers, careful not to burn them on the piping hot bits. The first course was followed by sweets in the shape of castles, made from almond paste. Next came platters of roasted goose and swan. The swans were a special treat. They had been stuffed with spices and sewn back into their feathered skins. All of this food was washed down with mugs of ale.

As Richard ate, he thought sadly that this might be his last banquet. He so wanted to complete his training and become a knight. Yet how could he? His brother's letter had instructed him to come home. Surely Lord Geoffrey had received the same message.

Afternoon

 blast of horns announced the start of the tournament. Richard's skin prickled with excitement as he watched the knights ride onto the field. Each was clad in gleaming armor and carried a flag with his coat of arms. Sir Kenneth's crest was green with a red lion.

There were four pairs of knights. Both Sir Kenneth and Sir Robert had won many such events. Richard knew that the skills used in jousting were the same as those needed for combat. In a jousting match, two knights on horseback used a variety of weapons to try and unseat each other. These matches could be dangerous and many knights had been severely wounded or accidentally killed.

This was the first event of the season and excitement was high. All the lords and ladies of the castle were in the grandstand. Sometimes a lady would hand her handkerchief to a favorite knight and he would tuck it into his armor. This was all part of the chivalry practiced by noblemen and noblewomen. From the corner of his eye, Richard saw Catherine hand her handkerchief to Henry.

Lord Geoffrey stood, raised his hand and then dropped it, signaling for the joust to begin. There would be three tries with a lance, then with swords and, finally, axes. Richard knew that the winner of this round would go on to fight the winner of the next round, and so on, until a victor emerged. He hoped that would be Sir Kenneth.

The crowd roared as two knights raced across the field, lances pointed at each other. The men passed without either being unseated. They turned their horses and repeated the move. Again, each remained on his horse.

"I bet on the knight on the black horse," said Henry.

Richard turned. "No, the knight on the gray horse is stronger."

"What will you bet?"

"The handkerchief that Catherine gave you."

Henry gave him a sly grin. "All right, it's a bet."

They turned as the knights charged.

"I win!" Richard jumped in the air. "My knight is seated while yours is on the ground." He held out his hand and Henry reluctantly handed him the scrap of lace.

"I shall win it back on the next round," said Henry.

Richard tucked the handkerchief halfway into his pocket. "I must go to Sir Kenneth. Tell Catherine I keep her favor close to my heart."

"Tell me yourself." Catherine appeared beside him. Turning to Henry she said, "And how will *you* win back my favor?"

"I will bet on Sir Robert."

"You would bet against Lord Geoffrey's favored knight?" Catherine feigned horror.

"For your token, I would bet against the King himself," declared Henry.

"The best knight shall win and that is Sir Kenneth," said Richard. "Now I must go to him." His heart pounded as he raced across the field. He stopped in front of Sir Kenneth, who was stroking Lion Heart. "Sir Kenneth," he said addressing the knight, "you *must* win."

"And why is my triumph so important to my young squire? Could it have anything to do with this piece of lace?" He touched Richard's pocket.

Richard's face flamed. Sir Kenneth laughed. "Ah, you are learning the art of chivalry all too well. Now help me don my armor."

Again trumpets blared as Sir Kenneth and Sir Robert raced at each other. Their lances touched, but did not unseat either man. One, two, three passes and each remained on his horse. After the third round, they returned to their corners. Richard took Sir Kenneth's lance and handed him a sword. "Use it well," he said.

Sir Kenneth turned his horse, paused, and then charged. Again, each knight remained seated.

Sweat beaded Richard's forehead. Sir Kenneth had to win! The joust entered its final stage. Richard picked up Sir Kenneth's battle-axe. Its blade was honed to a sharp edge. He shivered as he handed it to the knight.

Richard could hardly breathe. He knew that this was the time in a joust when accidents could occur. The fighting could become fierce. He watched with fear.

Sir Kenneth and Sir Robert had pulled so close that their horses resembled a single two-headed animal. Suddenly Lion Heart balked and turned abruptly to the left, sending Sir Kenneth tilting to the right. His hand holding the axe dangled over the horse's flank as his opponent reached out to shove him to the ground. Lion Heart swiveled. Sir Kenneth regained his balance, raised his arm, and—with a great burst of strength—swung his axe.

Evening

ord Geoffrey will be in a festive mood," Henry crowed as the boys returned to the keep. Indeed, it had been a thrilling finish. When Lady Anne awarded the prize of a gold medallion to Sir Kenneth, the people in the stands went wild. Everyone knew that Sir Kenneth was Lord Geoffrey's favorite knight and his win was a triumph.

"Yes, Lord Geoffrey will be in a cheery mood," Richard agreed.

"As will you." Catherine pointed to the lace protruding from Richard's pocket.

"My lady." He pulled it out and handed it back to her with a flourish. "You have made my day a triumph."

Henry scowled. "Enjoy your success while you can. For I shall soon win back the fair Catherine's favor."

Catherine tossed her curls and laughed. "And how shall you do that?"

"I will find a way," said Henry.

You won't have to, Richard thought, *for soon I will not be here to challenge you.*

Shortly after evening mass, a page summoned Richard to Lord Geoffrey's solar—his private chambers. Richard's feet felt as heavy as horse's hooves as he plodded along the stone floor. When he reached the solar, he took a deep breath and knocked on the door. A servant opened it and bid him enter.

Richard stepped into a spacious room dominated by a large four-poster canopied bed. It was covered with a red-and-gold brocade spread and two feather pillows encased in the same red-and-gold cloth. Several wooden chests lined the walls and a large stone fireplace faced the bed. Lord Geoffrey sat in an elaborately carved wooden chair before the fireplace. He wore a fur-lined robe and slippers, and his hair shone with reflected light from the fire. He motioned for Richard to step before him.

"Good evening, Lord Geoffrey." Richard bowed.

"Good evening, Richard," said Lord Geoffrey. "I hear good things about you from

Sir Kenneth. He did us proud in today's joust and I understand you had not a little to do with his success."

"I only polished his armor and groomed his horse."

"Yes, but a knight's horse and armor are like his arms and legs. Without them, he is helpless. Please, sit." Lord Geoffrey pointed to a short three-legged stool near his feet.

Richard sank onto it. Behind him flames danced in the fireplace, shooting showers of sparks into the air. In spite of the fire's warmth, he felt chilled to the bone. Soon, his life in the castle would be over.

"Richard, as you know, your father and I were comrades in arms," said Lord Geoffrey. "More than once he saved me from serious injury or death. I owe him a debt of gratitude. Since it was his wish that you become a knight, it is my desire to see his wish fulfilled."

Richard's head snapped up. Was he being told that he could stay?

Lord Geoffrey continued. "I will notify your brother that you will remain here, as my ward, while you complete your training for knighthood."

Richard sprang to his feet. "Lord Geoffrey, how can I thank you?"

"Work hard to honor the customs of our castle, and follow the knight's code of chivalry." He rose and placed a hand on Richard's head. "You remind me of your father. He was a good man. I pray that you follow in his path."

Back in his room, Richard stared out the open window. He was saved. His dream of knighthood would be realized in spite of his family's troubles.

"So, Squire Richard, I hear you will not be leaving us."

Richard whirled around. Henry stood in the doorway, an enormous grin splitting his face.

"How do you know that? In fact, how did you know I might be leaving?"

"I know everything that goes on in the castle." At Richard's incredulous look, Henry laughed. "Sir Geoffrey's servant told the stableman, who told the cook, and I overheard them while I was in the buttery."

"Why were you in the buttery?"

"I thought you might be hungry. You haven't eaten since mid-morning." Henry pulled his hands from behind his back. In one there was a loaf of bread; in the other a wheel of cheese. "Shall we eat to celebrate our continued rivalry? I *shall* win back Catherine's favor."

Richard laughed. "We shall see. But you know, you'll never beat me in archery."

"We shall see about that, too," Henry said, breaking off a hunk of bread and handing it to Richard.

Yes, Richard thought. *We shall see about it all because now I have time.* ∞

The sword was a knight's most prized weapon.

The Warrior Class

ENGLAND

Knights were great warriors who fought for their king, queen, and their nobles. They were powerful men who owned land called fiefs. They lived in castles with thick stone walls and moats to keep out invaders such as other nobles or people from other lands who wanted to take their land.

A Noble Life

To be a knight, you had to come from a noble family. Knights swore an oath to their lord to fight for him for forty days a year. In exchange, the lord gave the knight land to build a manor house. That

Each squire was the devoted assistant to one knight.

made the knight a vassal, which meant he oversaw peasant farmers who worked at his manor. Peasants, or serfs, were at the bottom of the social ladder. They paid taxes to their lord and had to do what he told them. Peasants could not leave their land without their lord's permission. This system is called feudalism.

Years of Training

It took many years of training to become a knight. A boy from a noble family was sent to another noble's castle to become a page, or personal servant, when he was seven years old. Pages were taught how to use a sword and ride a horse. They were also taught good manners and how to act around lords and ladies.

Becoming a Squire

When a page turned twelve, he became a squire. He was assigned to one knight who taught him to fight in battle. In return, the squire cared for the knight's horse and armor and kept his weapons in good condition. The word "squire" comes from the French word *escuyer,* which means a person who carries a shield. One of the squire's jobs was to carry his knight's shield when he rode into battle. The boy remained a squire until he turned eighteen and then, if he proved he was ready, he became a knight. By then,

England
1197

Atlantic
Ocean

N

Scotland

Edinburgh

Northern
Ireland

Ireland

Dublin

Wales

KINGDOM OF
ENGLAND

London

English Channel

France

Throughout the medieval era, there were many wars between the Kingdom of England and neighboring tribes from Scotland and Ireland. Eventually, they would become the countries of England, Scotland, Wales, Northern Ireland, and the Republic of Ireland.

Chivalry

Knights followed a code of behavior called chivalry. The word comes from the French word *chevalier*, which means knight. Squires learned the code from instruction books and by watching other knights. They had to be polite, use good manners, treat ladies with respect, and never intentionally kill another knight, especially if he was unarmed. A knight also had a great responsibility to protect the Church,

he had learned to use large weapons—such as a lance, long sword, and a battle-axe—and to charge at an enemy. Jousting was a good way to practice these skills. In a jousting tournament, mounted knights in full armor charged at each other. Each one tried to knock the other off his horse. These jousting tournaments could be quite fierce, and knights were often hurt or even accidentally killed.

be brave and loyal, stay fit and healthy, and always act in an honorable way. A knight collected taxes from his serfs, and acted as a judge in court cases. He married a lady from a noble family. When his children were seven years old, he would continue the knightly tradition by sending each of them to another noble's home to begin their training to become knights or ladies.

Kame's Dispute

KAMAKURA, JAPAN, 1205

Morning

Good morning, Mother."

The *shoji* screen whispered as Kame slid it open and entered the room where her mother, Aya, was already eating breakfast. Kame saw that her mother's usually serene face was marked by a deep crease in her forehead. She looked worried.

Uncle Sawai was here last night, Kame thought. Every time her father's brother visited he brought anger into the house. Uncle Sawai and his greedy brother Yoshi wanted the land that Kame's father, Narishige, had left for Kame and her mother when he died.

Her mother looked up from her meal at her daughter.

Kame sat on a straw mat and studied her mother. In spite of her appearance— slender with delicate features—Aya was a strong warrior. Trained by her own mother, she was a skilled horsewoman and could use her bow and arrow as well as most men— a skill she had used to defend her family. She was wounded in her last battle, the one in which Kame's father was killed, and now, her right arm hung limp and useless at her side. Kame had begun to acquire skill in archery. But her mother no longer had the physical strength to teach her. Worse, she and her mother now had to deal with the uncles who wanted to throw them out of their own home. Her uncle wanted their house and lands for his eldest son. And he was using Aya's injury against her.

"Here is your breakfast," said Akiko, her mother's servant. She was bent over the *kamado*—the clay and mortar wood-fired stove where she cooked the family's meals. She had been Aya's nursemaid and came with her when she got married. Akiko wore a white cotton kimono and cotton leggings. Her face was wrinkled and her smile was warm.

"Thank you, Akiko." Kame accepted the bowl. She picked up her chopsticks and breathed in the fragrant aromas of steamed rice, miso, and paper-thin slices of sea snails called abalone. She sat across from her mother.

"Mother, what will you do about the uncles?" Kame leaned across the mat and looked into her mother's eyes. They were bright with anger.

"I will fight them." Aya set down her bowl. "I will go to the *shugo* to plead our case. He is in charge of our district and reports to the shogun. Your father was a loyal *goke-nin* and served his shugo and the shogun well. He died in battle, and now his brother wants to steal the rewards of his work."

Kame's father had been killed by relatives who called him a traitor for befriending a rival clan. It was the same fight in which Aya was wounded. A fierce rivalry had always existed between her father and his brother. Narishige had been an excellent horseman, skilled at both sword and bow and arrow. His fierceness in battle was legendary, as was that of his wife, who often rode beside him. His brother envied his good standing with the shugo and tried at every turn to cast doubts on his loyalty. Now that her father was dead, her uncle would turn the shugo against Kame and Aya. They would be forced from their home and deprived of their possessions—even Aya's armor.

> "Women have no place in this, and certainly not girls."

As if conjured from her thoughts, her uncle Sawai entered the room. He was tall with broad shoulders. He wore a dark kimono over wide black trousers and a *hitatare,* a short coat with wide sleeves and a string across the chest. His black hair was pulled back from his face and fastened into a ponytail that hung down his back. His sword was thrust through his *obi,* a broad belt that wrapped around his waist and tied in the front.

"Good morning, Kame." He turned and bowed to Aya.

"And to what do I owe the pleasure of this visit?" said Aya.

"Business," he sneered.

"I thought we settled that last night."

"Not to my satisfaction." He turned to Kame. "Leave us."

"No! Kame stays. This is her home, too."

"Women have no place in this, and certainly not girls."

"I had a place by my husband's side for fifteen years."

"And I am twelve and almost a woman," said Kame.

"Then stay if you will!" His hand rested on the hilt of his sword. He turned to Aya. "It was my brother's wish that our brother Yoshi and I care for you and Kame. We can do this best as overlords of this land. Your injury has made you ill equipped to run it. You have not been yourself since my brother's death."

"How would you have me be, with my husband slain through your lack of courage?"

Sawai's face turned red. "I stood by my brother's side."

"And ran when he was surrounded!"

"Would you that I were slain, too?"

"No! I would that you defended him; as I tried to do."

"And look what it got you. A broken body." He pointed to her twisted arm. "How will you lift your bow?"

"I will lift it for her." Kame stepped forward.

"Do not think more of yourself than you are worth!"

Aya jumped to her daughter's defence. "She is better equipped than you and your half-wit brother."

"Half-wit! Be careful what you say. Your words will come back to haunt you."

"Better to be haunted by the ghosts of my husband's brothers."

"Are you threatening us?" Sawai slid his sword out of its sheath.

Kame trembled at the cruelty in her uncle's eyes. Could it have been her uncle who organized the fight that killed her father?

Her uncle replaced his sword. "I must go. I do not want to be late for my meeting with the shugo." He smiled a hard, cruel smile. "As the lord of this province, he has the power to decide the best course of action, which he will then report to the shogun. He will see the wisdom of my plan," he smirked.

Back in her room, Kame sank onto one of the round straw mats that covered the raised bamboo floor. A small white and gray bird sat on a beam serenading her. Kame loved her room, with its rice paper walls, colorful pillows, and low tables. Against one wall stood a small charcoal brazier and a lacquered wood chest that held her *futon,* or sleeping mat. How could her uncle think of taking this place away, of forcing her and her mother to live in his house while he gave their home and land to his son and his son's new wife?

The family's house consisted of several single-story buildings, including the living quarters, the kitchen, and storage houses, built around a central courtyard and garden. The buildings were made of wood and paper, designed to be cool during the hot, humid summer months. The building materials were lightweight and, in case of fire or earthquakes, the houses were easy to rebuild.

Kame entered the courtyard. This was her favorite place. A stone bench sat between two large cherry trees. In April, their pink blossoms had scented the air and now, in June, their leaf-filled branches provided shade. The day was hot. Kame was wearing her light summer robe. She held her bow. A quiver of arrows rested at her feet. Standing, she went to the far side of the courtyard where a target was nailed to a tree. Her mother had forbidden her to use the bow until she could resume her lessons. But Kame had been practicing in secret.

Lifting the bow, she fitted an arrow into the string, took a deep breath, aimed, and shot. The arrow flew straight and then at the final instant, veered to the right and fell to earth.

"I must do better." Kame pulled another arrow from the quiver and repeated her actions. This time the arrow whizzed through the air and hit the mark. Goke-nin warriors were trained not to show emotion but still Kame shivered with excitement.

"So you are practicing to replace your mother."

Kame jumped. Urakami, the family's stable boy, stood behind her.

"Why do you spy on me?"

He shrugged. "I was merely coming to find you. Your horse needs to be exercised. Shall I ride him or will you?"

Suddenly, Kame knew what she would do. "I will ride him. If my mother asks where I am, tell her I am giving my horse a workout." She picked up her bow and arrow and walked toward the stable. She had a plan.

Afternoon

ide like the wind.

That is what her father told her when he gave her a horse. Hikari was small with a steady gait. Soon the horse and Kame were like one. Now it sensed her urgency. Its ears pinned back and legs flying, Hikari pounded the hard earth as Kame urged it toward the shugo's house. Her bow and quiver of arrows were slung over the horse's back.

The uncles will not turn us from our home, Kame fumed. *I will not let it happen.* In the distance, she saw the shugo's compound and for a moment her courage wavered. Was she doing the right thing? Would the shugo laugh at her, a mere girl? But Aya had fought beside her husband against those who would usurp the shogun's power. Together they had helped turn back the enemy. Did this not demand a reward? *A reward I have come to collect*, she thought. Gathering her courage, Kame pressed her heels into the horse's side. It trotted toward the compound entrance. A guard stepped into their path. Kame pulled herself up tall and lifted her head. She looked into the guard's eyes.

"I am Kame, daughter of Narishige and Aya. I have come to see the shugo."

"Is the master expecting you?"

"I come on urgent business."

"Then I will announce you." He disappeared through the gate. Kame fidgeted. What if the shugo refused to see her? What would she do then?

The guard returned. "The shugo will see you."

Kame slid off Hikari's back. She reached for her bow. The guard stopped her.

"Do not bring your weapon into the shugo's presence."

Kame pulled back her hand. She followed the guard through the courtyard into a large airy room where the shugo sat cross-legged on a straw mat. Her uncle Sawai stood before him.

"What are you doing here?" Sawai glowered at her.

Kame lifted her chin. "I have come to address the shugo."

Her uncle stepped between them. "My Lord," he bowed. "I must apologize for my niece. She is a lowly girl who thinks she has the right to bother a great lord with her childish demands."

Kame took a deep breath and bowed. "My Lord," she said, willing her voice to be steady. "I have come to plead for justice."

The Shugo looked at her with interest. "And what, may I ask, does this justice entail?"

"My father bravely fought and died in your service. My mother fought beside him. Now my uncle seeks to deprive us of that which is rightfully ours—our home, our possessions, and," she shot her uncle an angry look, "even the armor my mother wore in your service." She reached into her robe and pulled out a document. "This is my father's will. It will tell you his true wish—that my mother and I continue to live in our home."

Her uncle snatched it from her hand. He unrolled the thin sheet of paper and studied the writing. When he looked up his black eyes were narrowed to slits. "As I thought, this is a forgery. It was not written by my brother's hand."

"It is not a forgery!" Kame fought to control her temper. "My father told us this was his wish and he gave the will to my mother for safekeeping."

"And how did you get it?" Her uncle sneered.

"I borrowed it." Kame turned to the shugo. "It is my father's true will."

"Is this true?" the shugo turned to her uncle.

"The child tells only half the story."

The shugo leaned forward. "Perhaps then, you will tell me the other half."

Kame watched her uncle as he composed his thoughts. When he spoke, his voice was as slippery as silk.

"My brother Narishige was a great warrior. His deeds of valor are legendary. In his last great battle he fought like a tiger. Alas," he lowered his eyes, "this effort cost him his life. Beside him, his wife, Aya, a great horsewoman and archer, was seriously wounded. No longer can she wield her bow to protect her home. Before the battle, I pledged to Narishige that, should anything happen to him, I and our brother, Yoshi, would care for his family. It is that duty I would now perform."

The shugo looked from Sawai to Kame. "Your uncle seems sincere. Besides," he stroked his chin, "your mother can no longer defend your home."

Kame's mind whirled. How could she counter her uncle's argument when he made it sound so logical? Her uncle wanted her land for his son and once he had it, Kame and her mother would become servants in her uncle's house. Kame could not let that happen. She stepped forward.

"*Shugo-tono*, I can defend our home."

"You!" her uncle hooted. "How? By telling the raiders to go away?"

The shugo raised a hand. When he turned to Kame, his eyes were kind. "I understand your desire to keep your home, yet I see your uncle's concern as well."

Kame lowered her head. She did not want the shugo to see the tears welling in her eyes. Tears were a sign of weakness. Yet he had dismissed her as a mere child and was now talking as if her uncle's stewardship over her and her mother was a foregone conclusion.

Suddenly she had an idea. She turned to the shugo.

"I wish to challenge my uncle to an archery contest."

"What?" The men stared at her.

Kame stared back. "You say that we are undefended. My mother is still strong and is learning to wield a dagger with her left arm. And I," she looked straight at her uncle, "have inherited her prowess with a bow and arrow."

Her uncle laughed. "You shoot at targets in your courtyard."

"And you left my father surrounded by his enemies!"

A shocked silence filled the room.

"How dare you accuse me of cowardice!" her uncle roared.

"Silence!" The shugo clapped twice and his servant appeared. "Set up targets in the orchard, outside the courtyard." He turned to Kame and her uncle. "Indeed, we shall settle the issue of defence with an archery contest. Then I will make my decision."

The orchard was bathed in sunlight. Kame faced the target, which was nailed to a cherry tree. She fitted an arrow into her bow, lifted the bow to her shoulder and aimed. The arrow hit the target to the right of center. Now her uncle took his turn. His arrow was true to the mark. He looked at Kame and smirked.

Kame shot a second arrow. This one flew straight and hit its target. Again it was Kame's turn to wait as her uncle fitted an arrow into his bow and then froze as the sound of horses' hooves filled the air. Kame whirled around as two armor-clad warriors thundered toward them. An arrow whizzed over her head and another thudded into the ground at her feet. Kame stood her ground, faced the invaders, and lifted her bow. A third arrow barely missed her shoulder. She felt its wind as it passed. Raising her bow, she aimed at the lead horseman. She was about to shoot when the shugo stepped in front of her. The warriors reined in their horses.

Kame looked from the horsemen to the shugo, who was looking at her. She turned to see her uncle cowering behind her.

The shugo spoke. "These men are my soldiers. They rode in at my request. You, Kame, reacted with strength and bravery. And you," he turned to her uncle, "hesitated. In a true battle, that hesitation can be the difference between defeat and victory."

Sawai lowered his head. "I only waited to ensure my arrow would not hit my niece."

"And yet your niece did not hesitate." The shugo put his hand on Kame's head. "Go home, child, and tell your mother that your lands will remain in your possession."

Evening

ow could you go to the shugo without telling me?" Kame and her mother were in the courtyard. Above them, the sky blazed with the last rays of the setting sun. Kame hung her head. Her mother rarely scolded her, but when she did, her words stung like arrows.

"When I saw that you were gone," she continued, "I worried you would get lost, or worse, be attacked by bandits."

"I had my bow and arrow."

"Why did you not tell me? And you took the will without my permission."

"You would have stopped me. I needed to show the shugo that we own this land and I can defend it. And I did."

Her mother sighed. "Kame, what will I do with you?" Her expression softened. "You are your father's daughter."

"And my mother's!"

"We still have to deal with your uncle." Aya's good left hand clutched her useless right hand. "He will use this condition as a weapon against us."

"I told him you were skilled at wielding a knife with your good hand."

"You said that?" Her mother laughed.

"I have seen you practice, and I know you will get stronger."

"And what of your uncle? Sawai will still make more trouble for us."

"We will deal with him. *I* will deal with him."

Later, in her room, Kame rolled out her sleeping mat as the events of the day flashed through her mind. She knew her uncle would want to get back at her for shaming him before the shugo. "We will be strong," Kame said into the air. Somewhere, she knew, the spirit of her father was watching over her. "*I* will be strong, Father, to defend that which you have won through your own bravery and sacrifice."

With that declaration she felt a sense of peace, stronger than any she had known since her father's death. Today had been a good day and there would be more to come. ∞

A New Government

Japan

Leading up to 1185, there had been much conflict in Japan. Then the forces of warrior Minamoto Yoritomo defeated the Taira clan at the Battle of Dannoura. Yoritomo provided protection for Japan's warriors, or *goke-nin*. In 1192, he was appointed *shogun*, which means "barbarian-quelling general." This made him the first leader of a new government in Japan—the Kamakura *bakufu*. Bakufu means a "tent government"—the shogun's office was in a tent!

Two Governments

At the time, the Emperor and the Imperial court in the city of Kyoto already ruled Japan. The bakufu, however, was a judicial government—it provided order and solved arguments between Japan's warriors. This system is called a dual system of government. Shogun Yoritomo named local officials, called *Shugo*, for each province. Shugo brought law and order to their provinces.

The Mongols

The Kamakura bakufu defeated the mighty Mongol Empire, which attempted to invade Japan twice. The Mongols' leader, Kublai Khan, had conquered nearby Korea in 1258. In 1260, he declared himself Emperor of China. He then sent representatives to Japan's Imperial court and demanded they surrender. Khan first launched an attack in 1274. In 1281, he sent an even larger fleet of ships to attack Japan. But the Shugo commanded the Japanese to build walls that prevented the Mongols from landing. After sailing off the coast of Japan for six weeks, the Mongol fleet was destroyed by a huge storm called a typhoon. The Japanese later called this typhoon *kamikaze*, or "wind from the gods." The bakufu lasted until 1333, when a civil war ended its rule.

Minamoto Yoritomo was the bakufu's first shogun, or leader.

Three Levels

To a Japanese person, there were three levels of society: equals, superiors, and inferiors. When talking politely to an equal or an inferior, people would say the family name and add -san, like this: *Watanabe-san.* To address a superior, they would add -sama to the name. For a lord, they added -tono. Children were raised to address equals politely and avoid being emotional in public. Even at home they were not to make loud noises—this made sense, since the houses were made of paper.

Strong Women

During the Kamakura period, women held high positions in their homes. They were respected for their strength and abilities. The mother controlled the household finances and supervised the domestic helpers. A woman could inherit property and some even served on guard duty. Wives of goke-nin brought up their children to respect the principles of courage. They fiercely protected their land and many learned to read and write.

The Family

Based on the home a family shared and the land they owned together, strong ties grew. Family crests were added to clothes for the first time. When a child became an adult, he or she had a coming-of-age ceremony. Male children took their name from part of their father's name and a godfather's name. Girls were often named after animals or flowers. The name Kame in this story means "turtle."

Green tea was brought to Japan from China in 1191.

The borders of Japan have remained mostly unchanged for hundreds of years.

Japan, 1205

Kofï's Adventure

TIMBUKTU, MALI EMPIRE, 1345

Morning

or my entire life, I will remember my first sighting of Timbuktu. It was just past dawn when the flat roofs of the great city appeared before me. One magnificent structure towered above them. I rubbed my eyes. Was I seeing a mirage or was this vision real?

I turned to my father. "What is that great building?"

"That, my son, is the Djinguereber Mosque. Is it not spectacular?" Father held up his hand to halt the caravan. He leaned over his camel's head and pointed. "Mansa Musa is a great leader who has built a magnificent city. He brought an architect, Al-Sahili, to Timbuktu to build the mosque." He smiled and his teeth flashed white in his leathery face. "Prepare yourself, Kofi. We are about to enter a very special place. Come." Father flicked his camel's reins. "We have business to conduct."

As my camel lurched forward I thought how happy I was to be traveling with the caravan. I had waited for this chance since the age of six, when I had waved goodbye as my father left on his yearly travels. "When can I go with you?" I had pleaded.

"When you are twelve years old and ready to become a man," my father had answered. True to his promise, here I was, riding beside him at the head of ten camels, each loaded with precious goods. My father, Jawal, is a trader. He travels from our home in Cairo to the great cities of Venice, Constantinople, and Damascus, where he gathers spices, cotton cloth, foodstuffs, and leather goods. He then crosses the great desert and goes to Taudenni, in the northeast corner of Mali. At this barren outpost in the Sahara Desert he trades much of his goods for the salt that is mined there from the ground. Salt is more precious than gold because people cannot live without it. It is needed to preserve food, such as meat, that otherwise spoils quickly. My father then travels to Timbuktu where he sells the salt, which the Mali Empire does not have, for gold, of which they have a great deal. This is what I have learned during the weeks of our desert crossing.

I should explain about our caravan. We travel under the protection of the Tuareg people. They are known as the Blue People of the Desert because of their striking blue robes. They control the trade routes that go through the Sahara. They are also known as fierce fighters, so traveling with them keeps us safe.

We approached Timbuktu from the southern edge of the Sahara. The mighty Niger River is a short distance away. My father told me that this location—where the great river and vast desert meet—make Timbuktu a natural destination for traders. As we neared the city, my father halted the caravan. While the Tuaregs set up their domed goat-skin tents, my father gathered samples of his wares and packed them into two big leather sacks.

"You and I will go to the house of Ibrahim the merchant." He then turned to Mazin, the head camel driver. "Stay here with the camels until we return."

How proud I was to walk beside my father, each of us carrying a sack of goods to sell. As we entered the city, he gestured toward a square house with a flat roof. "In my father's time," he said, "these houses were made only of mud. During heavy rains, the walls and roofs would wash away. But when Al-Sahili was brought to this city, he added wooden posts to all the houses. Do you know why he put in these posts?"

"To make the mud walls stronger," I suggested.

"Yes. The posts support them so they don't collapse."

I followed him into a dusty narrow alleyway.

I studied the structure with interest. Then I glanced to my left. "Father, look, is that the Djinguereber Mosque? Can we visit it?" The mosque's walls soared upward and the wooden posts in the pyramid-shaped roof reached out to me like beckoning hands. How I longed to see it up close.

My father shook his head. "Not today. Today we must conduct our business. Come, we must walk to the house of the merchant Ibrahim."

I followed him into a dusty narrow alleyway. We walked in silence until my father stopped in front of a grand house. I tilted my head and stared at the structure. The massive doors were of solid wood and decorated with hammered steel plates and finely detailed nail heads. The windows were latticed wood, painted red, and covered with bits of metal.

The door swung open. "*Salaam*, Jawal," said a heavyset man in a flowing white robe. "And what fine goods have you brought to enrich our lives on this visit?"

"*Salaam*, Ibrahim." My father bowed. "I bring dates from Egypt, spices from merchants in Venice, and..."

"And..." said the man, his round face breaking into a smile.

"SALT!" My father laughed.

"Salt!" Ibrahim clapped his hands. "Come in, my friend, and we shall do business."

He led us into the main room of his house. The floor was covered with richly patterned rugs, and pillows of the finest cotton were scattered against the walls. Ibrahim clapped his hands and a servant appeared. "Bring us refreshments," he ordered. "Please, sit," he motioned toward the pillows. "You are my honored guests."

Once drinks and sugared fruits had been served, Ibrahim and my father began talking business. It was at this point that my attention wandered. Sensing my restlessness, my father turned to me.

"Kofi, take a walk in the city and see what other merchants are selling. It will be good experience for you and good information for me."

Gratefully, I jumped to my feet. "Thank you, Father."

"Do not wander far and return before the next call to prayer."

As I walked to the door, I heard their talk resume. I had a whole hour to myself and the wonders of Timbuktu awaited me.

Afternoon

he day was hot. The road shimmered with that strange image that looks like water but is nothing more than a mirage caused by waves of heat. I wiped my face with my sleeve. It came away damp with sweat. I looked up at the sky. The sun had climbed midway from the horizon. If I wanted to see anything of Timbuktu, I thought, I had better make haste.

Automatically, my feet turned in the direction of the mosque. As I walked along the street, I studied the people I passed. Most were richly garbed in fine cottons that were dyed a rainbow of colors. The women were very beautiful with dark skin, eyes, and hair, but it was their manner of dress that fascinated me. Although they were Muslim, they did not exhibit a traditional womanly shyness and did not wear veils. A girl, not much older than me, looked me up and down, as if measuring me for new clothes. When her eyes reached my face, she smiled and tilted her head. I smiled back and hurried away.

I continued walking, past mosques, mud brick houses, and a stately building that I later learned was a university. I paused to watch a mason who was busily replacing tiles on the front of the building. This was the dry season and masons were repairing houses that had been damaged during the rains. The city's houses are covered with Timbuktu stone, a hard clay that is cut from clay beds and left to dry. This covering distinguishes the city's buildings from those of other towns in the region. Replacing the stones provides work for Timbuktu's masons.

The work of the masons fascinated me, but there was much more to see, so I resumed walking. As I rounded a corner, I thought I heard footsteps behind me. I turned, but saw no one. I walked farther. Again the footsteps echoed my own. Every time I stopped, they stopped. When I looked back I saw nothing. Then I turned a corner, stopped quickly, and the footsteps continued. Whirling around I confronted a boy about my age who practically tripped over his feet to avoid bumping into me.

"Who are you? Why are you following me?" I asked.

The boy stared at me, his black eyes wide. Then he darted into an alleyway and disappeared.

I continued my journey, traveling deeper and deeper into the city. Timbuktu is renowned as a center of great learning and in one vestibule I saw a group of Koranic scholars poring over their holy books. As I turned a corner, I came to a sudden halt. There in front of me was the great Djinguereber Mosque. I caught my breath. So grand a structure was it that even now, I can hardly describe it. I will try. It is a beautiful temple with earth-colored walls of Timbuktu stone and lime, and a majestic tower that soars to the heavens.

"A magnificent sight, is it not?"

The voice seemed to come from my feet. I looked down to see an old man, dressed in rags, sitting cross-legged in front of the mosque. Such a sight was he, with his turbaned head and scraggly gray beard. His hands, when they stretched toward me, were like claws of a bird of prey.

"Come, sit beside me." The clawed hand reached out and I recoiled. "You think I am a beggar; a thief who wants to rob you. Perhaps I am." The man cackled. "But I am also a storyteller. And in here," he tapped his head, "is a tale you want to hear of Mansa Musa's fabled journey to Mecca and to Cairo."

"I am from Cairo," I said, intrigued in spite of myself. "I have heard of this journey."

"Then come, my young friend, and I will tell you more." He patted the ground and I sat beside him, drawn in by his soft, hypnotic voice.

"Mansa Musa was already known as a great ruler when he set out for Mecca in the year 1324. He had brought people from the four corners of our land into one mighty nation. He is admired for his fairness and his judgment. Mansa Musa is a Muslim and many of his subjects are Muslims. However, he has not forced anyone to convert, and everyone in Mali is free to practice his or her own religion. As a devout Muslim, however, Mansa Musa set out to fulfill his duty to make a pilgrimage to Mecca. For the journey, he assembled a train of one hundred camels, each carrying hundreds of pounds of gold. He was accompanied by sixty thousand courtiers and servants. His senior wife, Inari-Kunate, had five hundred slaves and servants of her own. Everyone was richly dressed. Mansa Musa wore silk

> "You think I am a beggar; a thief who wants to rob you. Perhaps I am."

robes embroidered with gold thread. When his caravan stopped in Cairo, Mansa Musa's generosity flowed. He gave one thousand raw gold ingots to the emir—the city's leader—and large sums of gold to all the court officers.

He paused for breath. I said, "My father tells me that Mansa Musa brought a famous architect with him to change the buildings in Mali."

"Ah, that is the rest of my story. Al-Sahili is a scholar as well as an architect. It was he who built this magnificent mosque you see before you. And he introduced us to the art of using bricks for our houses so the rains do not wash them away. He also built Mansa Musa's palace in the capital city of Niani, in the south, on the Upper Niger River.

So entranced was I with the man's tale that I lost track of time. Suddenly I looked up. The sun had moved to the middle of the sky. My father would be looking for me. I jumped to my feet and, after thanking the storyteller and putting a coin into his hand, set out to return to the house. It was then that I realized I had no idea how to get back.

I struggled to get my bearings. Perhaps the storyteller could direct me. But when I looked for him, he was gone. A moment earlier the *muezzins'* call to prayer had filled the air and the streets were now empty. The air shimmered with heat. Sweat dripped down my back and puddled under my arms. I was lost. Where would I go? What would I do? Then I saw the urchin who had trailed me earlier.

"You!" I whirled on him. "Who are you?"

"Someone who knows the streets of Timbuktu as I know the palm of my hand."

"Why have you been following me?"

He shrugged.

Anger boiled in me. Then I calmed down. "You say you know the city. Can you lead me back to the house of Ibrahim the merchant?"

The boy held out his hand. "We will do business, yes?"

I shuddered. My father had taught me not to trust strangers. Yet I had been mesmerized by a ragged storyteller and now I was putting my safety into the hands of this rascal. Yet what choice did I have? I reached into my pocket and pulled out a coin.

The boy held up two fingers.

"One now; the other when we arrive," I said.

He pocketed the coin and began to walk. I followed him. Prayers were over and the streets were crowded again. The boy walked fast and I had to concentrate to keep up with him. Up one laneway and down the next; I looked for familiar landmarks but none appeared. Wherever he was taking me, this was a different route from the one I had previously traveled. I knew that under Mansa Musa, Timbuktu was safe compared to the lawlessness in other big cities. But I also knew that every city has its dangers and I was beginning to fear that this nameless boy was leading me into a trap.

All at once the boy stopped and turned to me with a sly grin. Then, without a word, he opened a door, darted inside, and bid me follow. I hesitated. What to do? I was now more lost than ever yet I dared not follow him into an unknown place. As I stood there planning my next move, a familiar voice boomed over my head.

"Kofi, where have you been? I was afraid you had gotten yourself lost."

I looked up into my father's angry face.

Behind him Ibrahim was frowning at the urchin. "Kazim, I told you to take Kofi to the mosque and then bring him back before prayers." He turned to my father. "I must apologize for my son. Too often he loses track of time."

Kazim! I stared at the boy in disbelief. "You are Ibrahim's son?"

Kazim's eyes sparkled. "Yes. Who do you think I am?"

"A robber; a beggar; an assassin." I threw up my hands. "How should I know when you creep after me like a thief?"

Ibrahim glared at his son. "Again you are playing games. And you are almost a grown man." He turned to me. "Did he ask you for money?"

"It was only in jest. I was going to give it back." Kazim fished the coin from his pocket and tossed it to me. "Tell the truth, Kofi. Wasn't it exciting to think that you were in danger?"

I burst out laughing. "If you had introduced yourself, we could have walked together instead of slinking through alleyways."

"Yes, but the slinking was more fun."

Ibrahim shook his head. "My wife has prepared a meal in honor of your visit to Timbuktu. Jawal, it will be my pleasure for you and Kofi to join us."

My father bowed. "The honor is ours. As for you, Kofi, I will talk to you later."

Kazim took my arm. "After the meal I will take you to a shop where they sell nothing but sweets. We can spend your coins there." He grinned. "The one I gave back to you and the one you still owe me for our safe arrival."

Evening

That night, after evening prayers, my father called me into his tent. "So, my son, you have had an interesting day. Sit and tell me what you have learned."

I settled myself on a silk cushion. The tent walls glowed with reflected light from oil lamps suspended from the tent poles. Before me was a brass tray filled with dates, figs, apricots, and almonds. From outside, I could hear a servant strumming a *guimbris,* a two-stringed instrument with a soft sweet sound. I looked up at my father. If I was expecting anger, I saw amusement instead.

"So Kazim played a trick on you."

"Yes, Father, but before he came, I *was* truly lost."

"That is why Ibrahim had him go with you. It seems, however, that Kazim is a prankster."

"As his father well knows." I smiled. "At dinner we became friends. Next time I will find a good trick to play on him."

"But tell me, Son. I sent you into the city to study the merchants and their stalls. What did you learn?"

"I admit, Father, that I found out little about the merchants. About the city of Timbuktu, however, I learned a great deal." And I proceeded to tell him about the storyteller and his tale of Mansa Musa's pilgrimage to Mecca.

"I was in Cairo when that caravan came through," said my father. "I saw the great ruler astride his camel. He gave away so much gold he lowered its value. That meant the money that traders like myself made for our goods was worth less than before. Still, he has done much good and I admire him."

"I do, too," I said. "Father, now that you have sold your goods, what will you carry on our return trip?"

"Gold. With that I will buy more goods, especially salt, and when I have enough I will come back. It is a good thing that we do, Kofi, for with all its wealth, Mali and its people could not survive without our salt."

I left my father's tent and stood in the middle of the campground. The camels had been fed and settled for the night. The goats were milked and our Tuareg guides were sleeping inside their domed tents. I knew I should do the same. But I was too excited. I walked to the edge of the camp, lay down on the sand, and looked up at the sky. A magic carpet of stars floated above my head. *Wherever I went in the world*, I thought, *these same stars would hover over me*. The thought was comforting. When I returned home, I would share the stories I had heard about Timbuktu and the ruler who spread gold over the land, as others spread honey on bread. Tomorrow we would water the camels and gather supplies to sustain us on our long journey back across the Sahara. Already I could feel the dry desert wind brushing my face. I smiled. The far trek would give me ample time to plan a trick to play on Kazim when I returned to Timbuktu. I could hardly wait. ∞

Timbuktu: A Center of Trade and Culture

THE MALI EMPIRE

Camels were the main source of transportation.

Timbuktu, which was part of the Mali Empire, was an important trading post because of its location at the exact point where the great Niger River flows into the southern edge of the desert. It was called "the point where the camel meets the canoe." It was in Timbuktu that people gathered to trade goods from West Africa, North Africa, and the Mediterranean, and where salt was traded for gold.

An Empire is Born

The Mali Empire began as a small kingdom of the Malinke people. It was conquered by the Sosso people under King Sumanguru. Sumanguru wanted to make sure no one would steal his throne so he killed eleven of his twelve brothers. The twelfth, whose name was Sundiata, fled and came back with an army that defeated Sumanguru in the Battle of Kirina in 1235. Sundiata moved his capital to Niani, which is

Mansa Musa was the tenth ruler of the Mali Empire.

on the Niger River. This made Timbuktu, also on the Niger, an important trade center as many people traveled along the river. His son Mansa Uli captured Timbuktu and added it to the Mali Empire.

A Great Leader

Mansa Musa was the Emperor of Mali between 1312 and 1332. He expanded Mali and built it into a strong and wealthy nation. Timbuktu had three universities and one hundred and eighty Koranic schools. Its Islamic scholars were renowned throughout the world. Their buildings were beautiful and their people were well kept. Education was highly prized.

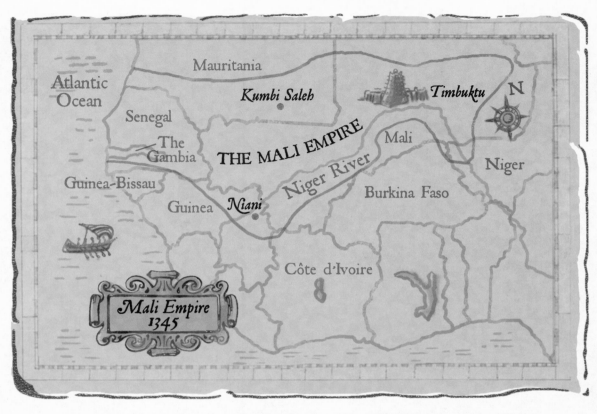

The Niger River helped to connect Timbuktu to other African cities of that time, such as Niani.

Golden Journey

In 1324, Mansa Musa made a lavish 9,600 km (6,000 mile) round-trip pilgrimage to Mecca. He took with him 60,000 porters, each carrying 3 kg (6.6 lbs.) of pure gold. He had so much gold that when he distributed it in Egypt, the Egyptian currency went down in value. On his return to Mali in 1330, he brought the famous Spanish architect Abu Ishaq Ibrahim Al-Sahili back with him. Al-Sahili built two magnificent buildings in Timbuktu—the Djinguereber Mosque and Madugu, the royal palace. Timbuktu became known as "the pearl of Africa."

Timbuktu Falls

Mansa Musa was a great ruler and kept his kingdom peaceful and prosperous. His descendents continued to rule until 1434, when Somi Ali Ber of the Songhai Empire captured the city. In the 1500s, Moroccan armies from the northwest of Mali invaded and sacked Timbuktu. They killed many people and destroyed the city's mosques and schools. Then the old caravan routes, which were the source of Timbuktu's power, shifted eastward. Today, the once magnificent city is a dusty town and few people know of its former glory.

The Stowaway

VENICE, 1351

Morning

arco hurried along the canal. It was still dark but he was too excited to stay in bed. Today his uncle Antonio, the best ship outfitter in Venice, would oversee the launch of his newest vessel. And he, Marco Morosini, was going to be on it.

Of course, no one knew about this—it was Marco's secret.

Five years ago, in 1346, his father, Carlo Morosini, had sailed away to the East on a ship captained by Giorgio Marin. His father had planned to bring riches from that land back to Venice and sell them for a handsome profit. Captain Marin and his ship returned. Marco's father did not.

Then in 1349, when Marco was ten, the Black Death struck Venice. Thousands of people died—half the population of the city—including Marco's mother. Marco was left an orphan, so his uncle adopted him. Since then, Marco had spent a great deal of time at his uncle's factory in the Arsenal, the manufacturing district on the eastern side of Venice where all the great ships were built. It was from here that his uncle's newest ship was being launched. And none other than Giorgio Marin was to be the ship's captain!

Marco stepped aside as two well-dressed gentlemen swished past. They were rich. He could tell from the finely tailored lines of their cloaks and their hats. They wore leather boots with high heels that raised them above the garbage that was rotting in the street. The cloak of one of the men brushed Marco's leg as they passed. He jumped. It was not unknown for a rat or two to scamper over one's feet. Regaining his composure, Marco stared at the men's backs. *I will dress like that when I return from my travels.*

He regarded his reflection in the water of the canal. His clothes were simple—a cotton shirt and wool pants. His toes were cramped against the tips of his sturdy but scuffed shoes. "I will be a gentleman," he said to the dark-eyed boy staring back at him from the water's surface. "I must get on that ship."

The sky had lightened to a pale blue with streaks of orange clouds. *A beautiful day*

to sail, thought Marco. He did not know where Captain Marin's ship was going but it did not matter. Egypt, Syria, Constantinople, Flanders, or England—all would hold the riches that Marco desired. And at least one port of call, he hoped, would yield the answer to his father's disappearance.

He resumed walking. Venice was a series of small islands divided by canals. To get around, people walked on the streets that ran alongside the canals. Bridges crossed the canals, connecting one island to the next. Many people traveled by boat, mostly in the long narrow gondolas that glided through the water.

How lucky he was to live in Venice, the trading center of the world. Here great galleys were built, outfitted, and launched to sail the seas. The Venetian government organized several *mudas*, or convoys, to sail from Venice each year. In order to place cargo on a ship, a merchant had to be a resident of Venice. The mudas carried salt, olive oil, beeswax, wood, and grain to the exotic ports of Marco's dreams. There they filled their holds with spices from India, silk from China, cloth from France, cotton from Egypt, and foodstuffs from Constantinople. These treasures were sold to merchants who came to Venice from all over Europe and countries in the East because they knew that whatever they were seeking, they would find it here.

Marco turned along the Grand Canal, the main waterway that ran through the city's core. Even at this early hour, traffic was heavy. He watched a gondola piled with wooden coffins glide by and shuddered. He saw this sight often during the Black Death. Marco scurried back to the footpath beside the canal. If he didn't hurry, he would miss the launch and his chance to sail with Captain Marin. He quickened his steps. The path was crowded with people on their way to market, merchants going to their places of business, and children scampering through the crowd. Although Venice was a rich and powerful city, there was also great poverty and Marco saw many a ragged wretch with hands outstretched to passersby.

As he walked, Marco marveled at the beauty of his city. Buildings were made of brick and the structures sat on layers of stout wooden poles that had been driven down under the water. The outsides of many houses were painted or plastered and some had been decorated with paintings of family crests and coats of arms. Some windows were covered with colorful awnings and balconies displayed washing hung out to dry.

When he finally arrived at the Arsenal, it was a hive of activity. About two thousand people worked here, building and outfitting the ships that made up Venice's naval and merchant fleets. A high windowless wall surrounded the entire complex. Marco entered through the only doorway—a security measure that kept unwanted people out. The guard recognized him and waved him through. He passed dozens of warehouses and long brick sheds. Each shed housed a ship under construction. Uncle Antonio's was at the far end of the vast complex. All the ships were built by people who worked for the Venetian government, but private companies were allowed to outfit and maintain them. Marco's uncle owned such a company and had installed the masts and riggings that held the ship's sails.

"Hello, young Marco." A worker waved to him from inside his uncle's shed. Marco entered and stared at the giant craft. It was called a great galley. The body was long and sleek with openings in its sides for a hundred oars. The ship could either be rowed or moved by sail, and it was so fast that it could travel from Venice to England in less than one month! Marco could not imagine anything moving with such amazing speed.

How lucky he was to live in Venice, the trading center of the world. Here great galleys were built, outfitted, and launched to sail the seas.

"It will hold a rich cargo," said his uncle Antonio. "I am sending a shipment of fine wine on this voyage. It will bring a handsome profit." He rubbed his hands together. In addition to outfitting the ship, he was also a merchant profiting from its journey.

"So, my lad, are you ready to watch the launch of the greatest ship ever to leave Venice?"

"Yes, Uncle." Marco looked at the man who was like a father to him. *I have three daughters who are the light of my life, but a man needs a son*, his uncle had said when he brought Marco home after the boy's mother died. Antonio's wife, Veronica, had accepted Marco without question. Antonio, too, had never been satisfied with Captain Marin's story that Marco's father had simply left the ship one morning and not returned. Marco knew that his uncle suspected skulduggery, but had never been able to prove it.

So I must do it, Marco thought as he watched the massive ship being prepared for the journey from the Arsenal to the sea. *I owe it to my father and when I return with an answer, my uncle will be proud of me.*

He had left a note on his bed telling his uncle and aunt of his plan, so they would know where he had gone. Yet, he knew they would fear for him and that made him sad. On the other hand, his destiny was to learn of his father's fate.

"Such deep thoughts?" Antonio tapped his shoulder. "Come. Let us board the galley one last time before its journey out on the open sea."

"I would like that, Uncle." Marco followed him up the gangplank of the ship. Once on board, he looked around the deck, searching for hiding places. Soon it would be time to put his plan into action.

Afternoon

The polished wood of the ship glowed golden under the noonday sun. Marco felt proud. His part had been small, helping his uncle polish the masts. What fun that had been, shimmying up and down the posts. Now they stood tall and proud, pointing to the cloudless sky. He stood by the rail while his uncle spoke with Captain Marin. The captain was always nice to Marco. Perhaps it was guilt for orphaning him. *Will he still be kind when he finds me as a stowaway?* thought Marco.

The thought made him shiver. He knew he was taking a big risk, but it was something he felt to the bottom of his soul that he must do. Soon the ship would leave the Arsenal and enter the Venetian lagoon. From there it would go around the Lido and enter the Adriatic Sea. Somehow, he had to hide until the ship was too far out to sea to be brought back to land if he were to be discovered.

"Marco, it is time to disembark." Marco jumped as his uncle touched his shoulder.

"Yes, Uncle." Marco bid Captain Marin farewell and walked to where the gangplank had been lowered. The people who had come on board to outfit the ship had already disembarked. Marco and his uncle were the last to leave. As they stepped onto the dock, Uncle Antonio stopped to speak to a group of workers.

Marco tugged at his uncle's sleeve. "Look, it is my school friend, Mario. He has something to tell me." Before his uncle could react, Marco darted into the crowd. He looked back to make sure his uncle wasn't watching and then doubled back to the ship. Bending low to make himself small, he scampered up the gangplank just as it was raised from the dock. A quick glance assured him that in the bustle of departure, no one had seen him. He scuttled over the deck, and descended into the bowels of the ship.

Here, in the belly of the ship was a dark world, so different from that of the sun-drenched deck he had just left. He was standing in the hollow space where the ship's rowers sat. On either side were fifty shirtless men clutching the handles of the hundred oars that would propel the ship.

Marco crouched in the corner. No one had seen him. The floor of the ship shuddered. Damp heat wrapped around him like a blanket. He felt a swaying motion as the giant vessel passed the Lido and entered the open water of the Adriatic Sea. He had often stood on the shore watching ships sail to distant lands. He closed his eyes and pictured what was happening up on deck. The giant oars slapping the water; the massive sails unfurling overhead to catch the wind. He tried to recall the tangy smell of the sea, as it would be up on deck, instead of the stench of sweaty bodies crammed into a cramped, hot space.

The swaying of the ship and the heat soon overcame him. Marco closed his eyes and drifted off to sleep.

Evening

A thick meaty hand clamped Marco's shoulder. "Wake up, boy! What are you doing here?"

He looked up into the angry eyes of the foreman.

"I, I…"

"A stowaway, are you?" the man snapped. "The captain won't be happy about this." He pulled Marco to his feet. Turning to the rowers who were hunched over their oars, he bellowed, "What will we do with the lad, men? Toss him overboard?"

"I think he'll make a scrawny meal for the fish," shouted a rower from near the front.

"Even a scrawny meal is better than none," a second rower laughed.

"No!" Marco tried to stand but his foot was caught in a coil of rope and he felt himself lurching forward. "No!" He steadied himself by putting a hand on a cask and disentangling his foot. "Please, don't throw me overboard."

"Shall we keep him down here?" said the foreman. "Attach him to one of the oars."

"That'll strengthen him up right fast enough," said a rower.

More laughter. Marco watched their backs moving forward over the oars and then back; forward and then back. Their arms bulged with muscles; sweat coated their skin. "Take me on deck. Captain Marin knows me. He'll tell you I'm not just a stowaway."

"Not just a stowaway?" The foreman scowled. "Then what are you?"

Marco pulled himself up to his full height. Calming himself, he announced, "I am Marco Morosini. My uncle helped build this boat."

"And you think that gives you the right to steal a ride?" The foreman poked his finger into Marco's back. "Up to the deck with you and we'll let the captain sort this out."

"What were you thinking?" Captain Marin roared. "Do you know that stowing away is a crime? I could put you in irons. I could toss you overboard!"

Marco shrank against the wall of the ship, wishing he could make himself invisible.

> ## "A stowaway, are you? The captain won't be happy about this."

"Do you have any idea how upset your uncle must be?" The captain's face was crimson; his eyes bulged as if they would pop from his head. He raised his lantern to get a better look at Marco. To the west, the last streaks of sunset painted the sky a fiery red. Marco craned his neck to see the evening stars high overhead. He had slept through the first hours of sailing; it was too late for the captain to turn the ship around. That had been Marco's plan; however, now he wondered if he had done the right thing.

"What were you thinking?" Captain Marin repeated. He brought the lantern closer to Marco's face. "Explain yourself."

"I, I, I…"

"Speak up, boy!"

"I wanted to sail with you so I can find my father," Marco blurted out.

"My word!" The captain slapped his forehead. "And what, young Marco, makes you think you will find him while sailing on my ship?"

"He disappeared while he was on one of your ships. I wish to search the ports."

"And which ports are those?"

"Wherever you dock." Marco squared his shoulders. "My father is in one of them."

Captain Marin sighed. "It is not that easy. Come into my cabin and we will talk."

Marco followed the captain through a door into a small but well-appointed room. Beside it, a wooden desk held maps and a large leather-bound book. Marco saw a glass box that held a needle attached to a pin. He walked over to look at it.

"That is a mariner's compass," said the captain. He joined Marco and pointed to the box. "It is the instrument that tells us which way the ship is going. The wind rose, or compass card, is attached to a magnetized needle. See," he pointed, "that's it on the end of the pin. The pin is resting on a hinge. The box itself is fastened down so it can't move. It stays in a position in line with the keel of the ship. Whenever the ship changes direction, so does the pin. By watching it, we can tell which direction the ship is going."

Whew, Marco whistled. He bent closer. "Look, Captain Marin. The pin is moving."

"Close your eyes," said the captain. "Do you feel the motion of the ship?"

Marco not only felt the ship swing, he heard its boards groan with the effort.

"The wind is picking up." The captain lifted his head. "I must go down and make sure everything is in order. I have not yet decided what to do with you."

"Let me come with you." Marco turned pleading eyes on the captain. "I will not be any trouble, I promise."

"You have *already* been trouble." Captain Marin paused and stroked his chin. "We will stop in Ancona early tomorrow morning. I will put you ashore there and hire a messenger to return you to your uncle in Venice."

"But then I will never find my father."

Captain Marin pulled out a chair. He motioned for Marco to sit and he took a chair on the opposite side of the table. "Marco, I do not know what happened to your father. I took ill on that voyage and was confined to my cabin for several weeks. The ship's doctor thought it might be the smallpox, so no one was allowed to see me. By the time I recovered, your father was gone. I questioned the first mate, who had taken over my duties, and then the rest of the crew. No one knew what had happened. Your father kept to himself, so it was awhile before anyone even realized he was gone. Not very good of the crew, but understandable."

"What do you think happened?" asked Marco.

"I think your father ran afoul of someone in Alexandria in Egypt. He had dealings with a cotton merchant there—a man with a shady reputation. I warned your father, but he assured me the situation was well under control." He paused. "I fear he was wrong."

"So I will not find my father?"

"No, I fear you will not. But you are a valiant young man to try."

"Then you are not angry that I stowed away?"

Captain Marin sighed. "You are impertinent as well as valiant—and lucky, this time. Another captain might not be so forgiving. Do not do this ever again!"

The ship swayed sharply.

"The wind is turning. Come out to the deck and see how we handle the riggings. You must know these things when you are a great sea captain."

"What makes you think I will be a captain?"

Captain Marin winked. "I see the way you look at that compass, as if it were made for your pleasure. And I see your eyes light up when I speak of riggings and masts and foreign ports. You, my boy, have the soul of a seafaring adventurer."

Marco followed the captain onto the deck. The wind had indeed picked up and the sails were slapping against their masts. He watched the sailors at work, tightening ropes, securing loose objects, all the while calling to each other over the howl of the wind. Now the ship was rocking back and forth. *Like a baby in its cradle*, Marco thought.

He turned to stare out at the water. It was dark and inky. Ahead, sea and sky became one. Where the invisible horizon ended, the stars began, crowds of light splashed across the vast blackness of the sky.

Marco thought of his father. Was Captain Marin telling the truth or hiding something of which he was ashamed? Had his father truly come to a bad end? Or would he reappear one day, a rich man at long last returned from his trading voyage? And what of himself? Was the captain right? Did he have the soul of a seafaring adventurer? Marco looked back at the sea. What wondrous mysteries lay on its many shores?

A bell sounded that it was time to eat. Suddenly, Marco was famished. Reluctantly, he turned away from the water. The sea would be there tomorrow and all the other tomorrows he would hopefully spend on ships. But first he must go home and face his uncle. *How would he do that?* he thought, as he followed the crew into the galley. He would do it, he decided, by telling his uncle the truth. His uncle might be angry at first, but he would understand Marco's desire to find his father. And though Marco may have failed there, he had discovered something just as important—a future for himself. ∞

Today, the city of Venice is a part of the country of Italy.

A Mighty Arsenal

THE REPUBLIC OF VENICE

The city of Venice is built on one hundred and ten low islands. Poles driven into the muddy ground beneath the water support buildings. Venice was once a part of the Byzantine Empire but in 697, the Venetians became their own republic. They elected a *Doge*, or duke, who ruled along with the *Maggior Consiglio*, or Great Council. This is the longest-lasting republic in history at one thousand and one hundred years.

Salt Riches

In a time before refrigerators existed, salt was important because it preserved food. The Venetians learned to harvest salt from the sea and trade it with people on the mainland for grain and wine and other food. In the early 11th century, Venice began to trade with Asia. Venetians needed ships to do this, so Venice became a major shipbuilding center. Ships were built in a huge complex called the Arsenal.

Great Shipbuilders

The Arsenal was divided into six units. One unit had sawmills and carpenters' shops where the ships' hulls were built. A second unit filled any cracks or openings in the ships to make sure they were waterproof. There were departments for making sails and manufacturing ropes and oars. There was also a building for making anchors and cannons, and a bakery for baking sailors biscuits to eat at sea. The people who worked in the Arsenal were privileged workers, and many of them also served as the Doge's bodyguards.

Marco Polo is one of the most well-known explorers in history.

Marco Polo in China

By 1271, Venice was a great trading city, rivaled only by the Italian cities Genoa and Pisa. That year, merchant and explorer Nicolo Polo and his brother, Matteo, set off on a journey to Asia. Matteo brought his seventeen-year-old son, Marco, with him. They returned from China to Venice in 1295 and brought with them many exotic goods and riches. Marco Polo wrote of these travels and was the first European to describe life in China and Japan.

Surviving Plague

In 1347, the great plague, or Black Death, struck Venice and killed half its population. In 1382, this plague returned. But by 1400, Venice had recovered and entered its Golden Age. Venice controlled the water routes to the East, and had trading posts throughout the eastern Mediterranean Sea. The Venetians built a special ship, the great galley, which could serve as both a merchant and war ship. It held two hundred tons of cargo, many cannons, and was staffed by two hundred sailors.

An Italian Treasure

Today, Venice is a part of Italy and a popular tourist spot. However, the future of this great city is threatened by pollution and some believe it may be sinking. The Italian government is committed to preserving Venice so that future generations may enjoy this unique and beautiful city.

The gondola pole is a famous symbol of Venice.

Pedro's Choice

TOLEDO, KINGDOM OF CASTILE, 1395

Morning

My name is Pedro Sanchez. I am thirteen years old and I am an apprentice woodworker. My master is Alfredo Mendes, a very skilled craftsman. We live in Toledo, the most beautiful city in the world. Toledo is in the Kingdom of Castile. My family has lived here for hundreds of years.

I had always thought I would learn my trade from my father, who was a brilliant wood carver, as was his father before him. But last year my father died tragically when a beam fell on him while he was building. I was then apprenticed to Señor Mendes and, as is the custom, I moved into his house. I will live here until I finish my apprenticeship, perhaps five or six years from now. While I earn no money, I do receive room and board. This helps my mother, as there is one less mouth to feed at home. My eldest brother, Manuel, has finished his apprenticeship and is now a journeyman, so he makes a daily wage that he gives to our mother to help care for herself and our sister, Teresa.

Our family is Christian. We have been Christian since the Romans conquered this area almost one thousand years ago. We even remained Christian during the five hundred years of Muslim rule. During that time, I am told, Muslims, Christians, and Jews lived together in peace. Art and architecture flourished and many great buildings, such as the Alcázar royal palace in Seville, on which my grandfather worked, were erected.

However, since the anti-Jewish riots four years ago, life has changed. That was when the Christian Spaniards of Seville, who had previously lived peacefully with their neighbors, went on a rampage and massacred hundreds of Jews. The riots spread to other cities and now Jews all over the kingdom live in fear. I have even heard rumors that Señor Mendes and his family are *conversos*—secret Jews. Today, that is a dangerous thing to be. If it is true, I worry that one day I will be forced to reveal their secret.

Since I have come to live in their house, the Mendes family has always appeared to be devoutly Christian. They go to church every Sunday. They eat pork and on Fridays, as is the rule, they eat no meat at all. Señora Mendes, a kind woman who longs for children, prays to the Virgin Mary every day. So why am I suspicious? It is a shadowy feeling that I do not understand. Señor Mendes is a skilled craftsman who will train me in a trade I will use for the rest of my life. He is a senior member of the woodworkers' guild and leads his guild members in parades on religious festival days. He is a very important person, so why do I continue to have these dark thoughts?

Today, I am going with Señor Mendes to the cathedral. It is a grand structure with magnificent tiles and intricate woodwork. We are bringing a new olive wood crucifix to install above the altar. As I dress, I look at the furniture in my room—all of it made by Señor Mendes. My favorite piece is the large mahogany chest, inlaid with dark brown leather that is secured with ornate nail heads. This chest holds all my possessions—my rosary, the good leather tunic I wear to church on Sundays, and the cloth tunic I wear during the week. I dress quickly because the morning is cool.

So why am I suspicious? It is a shadowy feeling that I do not understand... why do I continue to have these dark thoughts?

When I am ready I join Señor Mendes in his workshop.

"*Bueños dias*, Pedro. Are you ready for our adventure?"

"Yes, Señor Mendes." I walk over to the bench where he is wiping sawdust from the new cross.

He holds it out for my inspection. "It is perfect, yes? And we will deliver it in good time for the Easter celebration."

I take it in my hands. It is as tall as I am and half as heavy. "It is beautiful." My heart jumps in my chest. This cross will hang over the altar in the cathedral, and when I am on my knees, I will look up at it and glow with pride, knowing that I have had even a small part in its creation.

As we leave the house, Señor Mendes places his hand on the doorframe. I have seen Jewish homes with pieces of wood nailed to the doorpost. I am told they contain a prayer. Could this be why my master touches his doorpost as if offering a blessing? This is one of his gestures that I do not understand. He does this every time he enters and leaves his home. I have never asked him about it because I am not sure I want to know the answer.

The sunny day is perfumed with the scent of blossoming orange trees. Señor Mendes walks briskly, greeting people along the way. Baker Ramirez waves a floury hand as we pass his shop. The smell of fresh bread makes my mouth water. We then pause at the doorway of the butcher's stall.

"Señora Mendes has instructed me to order a pork roast to celebrate before the start of Lent," says Señor Mendes.

He disappears into the shop and I prop the cross against the wall. The week before Lent is the most exciting of the year. There is a carnival atmosphere. I see revelers in huge masks. Fools ply the crowd with their antics while musicians strum instruments and passersby dance over the cobbles in the street. Two old women are deep in talk, their chins wagging up and down, straw shopping baskets slung over their arms. Two monks glide past, eyes downcast; their nut brown robes swish along the ground. I close my eyes to better feel the sun's warmth. The fresh spring air tastes like wine after so much time spent inside Señor Mendes's shop.

"Hello, cousin."

My eyes pop open and I see a tall boy in a soft leather tunic and boots swaggering toward me.

"*Bueños dias*, Juan. What brings you to this side of the city?"

"An errand. I am to pick up pork from the butcher. And what are you doing here?"

"I am waiting for Señor Mendes." I nod toward the butcher shop. "His errand is the same as yours."

"So your Jew eats pork! As if that will hide his true identity!"

I stare at Juan and the look in his hard black eyes sends a chill up my spine. "Señor Mendes is a good Christian."

"That is what you want to believe," he sneers. "I do not understand you. Even if I were starving, I would not work for a Jew."

"Señor Mendes is not a Jew! He is as good a Christian as you. Look," I point to the cross. "Would a Jew make such a beautiful object to give to the church?"

Juan laughs. "It will take more than a piece of wood to save his soul from the fires of Hell. Be careful, Pedro. Do not let his disease rub off on you."

Señor Mendes emerges from the store, rubbing his hands. "My wife will be pleased. I have ordered a fat pork roast that will fill her cooking pot to overflowing." He sees Juan and the color leaves his cheeks. "What do you want, you hoodlum?"

"And who are *you* to call *me* such a name?" Juan spits on the ground. "Be careful, old man. You will not be calling me names for long." He looks at me and smiles. "Remember what I said, cousin."

It takes a moment after Juan leaves for Señor Mendes to regain his composure. When we resume our walk, he is quiet. I steal a sideways glance at him. Is it my imagination or has my master aged in only a few minutes? I blink and the illusion is gone. Señor Mendes pauses to give a coin to a beggar and then we stop at the candlemaker's shop to buy a candle to light in the church. But the joy has left the morning.

Afternoon

We are back in Señor Mendes's workshop. Our visit to the cathedral was a success. The priest said our cross was the most beautiful he has seen. My master glowed with pride. He has recovered from our encounter with Juan, but I am still troubled. Could Juan's accusation be true?

"Pedro." I turn as my master enters the workshop. It is a long room with a wood table running down the middle. Woodworking tools hang in racks on the stone wall, and the wood plank floor is carpeted with sawdust. All of this is as familiar to me as my own hand. Yet today it seems strange. Juan has planted a seed of poison in my mind.

"See what I have." Señor Mendes places a solid block of wood on the table. "This is for you. I want you to practice the skills I have taught you and make a second cross for the small chapel at the church."

Is he avoiding my gaze as he speaks? I look at him. He is the same kind master I have known these many months, yet something has altered. At that moment Señora Mendes enters the room. She is short and plump with dark eyes and a ready smile.

"Pedro," she asks me, "I need water from the well."

"Woman, why do you ask my apprentice to perform such a task?" snaps Señor Mendes. It is odd to see him so agitated. He is normally so calm. "Have the servant do it."

"Maria has gone to the market for garlic and onions."

"Wait for her to return or get the water yourself."

Señora Mendes places her hands on her hips and glares at her husband. "I cannot leave my kitchen."

I step forward. "I will get the water and come back quickly. Will that do, Señor Mendes?"

"Go, go." He waves his hand but does not look happy.

I am happy to walk to the well in town. How I long to set down my empty bucket and dance with the carnival revelers. But I have made a promise, so I turn in the direction of the well. As I approach, I see a commotion. A young woman wearing the yellow band of a Jew is being pushed away by a group of rowdy boys. One shoves her too hard and she falls against the tiles, tipping over her bucket so the precious water spills into the street.

"Jewess! You are trying to poison the water."

"I am not." The girl tries to stand but the lout pushes her back down.

"Stop that." I race over and as he turns I see the angry face of Juan.

"If it isn't my Jew-loving cousin, Pedro." He waves at his companions. "Can it be that Pedro himself is a converso? He works for a Jew and now he defends one of them."

"You are an idiot, Juan." I give the girl my hand and help her to her feet. "I am no more a converso than you. This girl was not poisoning the well—she was merely drawing water, as I have come to do."

"You are such a naïve child," sneers Juan. "Soon it will be their Passover holiday. It is a time when Jews murder Christians—do you not know that?"

...as he turns I see the angry face of Juan.

As we argue, the girl tries to return to the well but the louts stand in her way. "Go home," I say softly. "I will make sure they do not harm you."

"Thank you," she whispers and, clutching her empty bucket, scurries off.

"Now, if you do not mind," I say, with more bravado than I feel, "I will fill my bucket and get back to work."

"Yes, go back to your Jew master." Juan's face is dark and ugly.

"I will return to the good Christian home where I am an apprentice to the finest woodworker in Toledo." I fill my bucket and as I walk away I hear Juan's voice.

"Take care, cousin, that you are not ensnared in the net that traps your master." His laugh follows me down the street until I turn a corner and leave it behind.

Evening

Back at the house, I give the water to Señora Mendes and return to the workshop. Señor Mendes is sanding a block of wood. He still seems preoccupied. True, it is Friday. I know that Friday night is the start of the Sabbath, an important time of rest for Jews. He is looking through the window. I follow his gaze and see that the sun is setting. In the kitchen, Señora Mendes clatters the lids of her pots. She has lit candles and their light casts a dusky glow. I also know that Jews light candles at the start of their Sabbath. But Señora Mendes lights candles every day as the daylight fades. So why should I think tonight different?

"Come." Señor Mendes turns from the window and sets down his tools. "It is time for our supper."

We take our places at the long wooden table. It is a beautiful piece of craftsmanship that Señor Mendes carved with his own hands. Made from a solid piece of cedar, the surface is as sleek and smooth as a piece of silk.

Supper is fish, as it always is on Fridays. Señora Mendes has cooked it with sweet peppers, garlic, and onions. The food is served in wooden trenchers, carved by Señor Mendes, and we eat it with large spoons. For dessert there is a *tortas de aceite*, a sweet olive oil pastry made with almonds. We wash the meal down with wine drunk from silver goblets. It is a fine meal and I compliment Señora Mendes, who beams with pleasure.

After supper, while Maria clears away the dishes, I walk outside. The night is clear and bright. I look up at a sky speckled with stars. Up and down the street our neighbors are finishing their meals and the sound of their voices drifts through the open windows. I close my eyes and think about the day. Juan's accusations have infested my mind, like a worm burrowing in an apple. Are the Mendeses conversos? And, if they are, why is that bad? Señor Mendes is a good man. His wife is a kindly woman whose great sadness is that she has never borne children. So she fusses over me as the son she never had. Yet people like my cousin would have me sneak around and spy on them. This is not something that I can do. But if they are secretly practicing their Jewish religion and I do not report them, will I be committing a great sin?

"Pedro, you will become ill standing here in the night air without a wrap." Señora Mendes hands me a wool garment. I take it and smile.

"You are like my mother. And you cook even better. The meal was delicious; the best I have ever had."

A smile of pleasure wreaths her face. "Come inside. I do not want to have to nurse you through a bad cold."

I follow her into the house. Its warmth envelops me. "*Buenos noches,* Señora. Where is Señor Mendes?

"He is in the workshop." She shrugs. "Even at night he cannot leave his wood alone."

I walk from the kitchen into the shop. My feet tread softly on the sawdust-covered floor. A lantern sits on the worktable where my master is

> **I close my eyes and think about the day. Juan's accusations have infested my mind, like a worm burrowing in an apple.**

bent over, his head in his hands. I hear him muttering under his breath in words that I do not understand. What I hear sounds like *baruch atta adonoi* and my blood runs cold. I know I have heard the phrase before—it is a Jewish prayer. As I approach his head snaps up and his eyes dart furtively from side to side.

"Pedro, I did not hear you come in."

"I only wish to bid you good night." I look into his eyes. "It seems you were talking to yourself."

"It was nothing. The mutterings of an old man." He pulls a cloth from his pocket and wipes his forehead. I remember the Jewish girl at the well. His face has the same hunted look I saw in hers.

"Some mutterings are better left unsaid," I tell him in a tremulous voice.

"Yes." He nods his head. "These are dangerous times for an old man's thoughts."

"And for those of a young man as well." I look deep into his eyes. "Perhaps we are all best served by silence."

Señor Mendes rises. He closes his eyes and I can hear his breath coming in slow measured beats. When he speaks, he is careful and controlled. "You are good and wise, Pedro. I trust you."

"And you are a good master. I am learning a great deal and wish to continue."

We nod at each other. We have reached an understanding.

I return to my room at the back of the house and shut the door. I sit on the oak chest. My fingers play with the brass studs that both decorate and hold it together. I think that, like them, I, too, am a fastener because it is in my hands to keep the Mendes family safe and together. To do this, I will keep my suspicions to myself and Señor Mendes will take care to hide his true religion. That way, I pray, we will all survive in this strange new world where villains like my cousin Juan threaten anyone who appears different from themselves. I smile. I meant what I said to Señor Mendes. I *am* learning a great deal— to be a woodcarver and also to be an honorable man. ∞

A Secret Life: The Conversos

The Kingdoms of Castile and Aragon

The Torah, the holy writings of the Jews, are on a scroll.

For centuries, the Jewish people lived in Canaan—what is today known as Israel, Lebanon and Palestine. But around 586 BCE, after the Babylonian King Nebuchadnezzar II conquered Jerusalem, Jews are thought to have moved to the Iberian peninsula. This is where Spain is today. The exiled Jews settled in and around the city of Toledo. For hundreds of years, they prospered under the rule of the Roman Empire.

A New Religion

Then, around 300 CE, Christianity became the official religion of the Roman Empire. The Christians blamed the Jews for murdering the Messiah. The Jews' lives became more difficult. In 306, Jews were segregated from the rest of society and forced to convert to Christianity or leave. In 711, Muslim armies invaded the area. The Jews welcomed them as liberators.

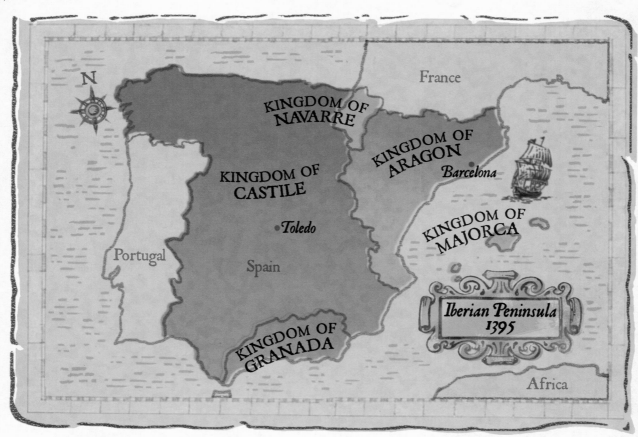

These kingdoms were all on the Iberian peninsula. Today, they have become the country of Spain.

Modern Spain was formed when King Ferdinand of Aragon and Queen Isabella of Castile married.

Great Freedom

Under Muslim rule, Jews enjoyed freedom and wealth. They served in government and were prominent in the arts. The time between 1000 and 1148 is considered a great period in Hebrew literature, with many Jewish scholars and writers achieving high status. Jews became successful in trade and crafts. They served as bankers, tax collectors, and physicians for the kings.

Attacks Come

Then, in 1391, life for these Jews changed again. Fanatic monks who wanted to destroy the Jewish influence in Spain organized a series of *pogroms,* or attacks. Hundreds of Jews were killed and many others were forcibly baptized as Christians. These people were called *conversos*— people who converted to Christianity. Although outwardly Christian, many conversos secretly continued to practice Judaism. This was very dangerous because if they were caught, they faced death.

The Inquisition

In 1478, King Ferdinand of Aragon and Queen Isabella of Castile were married, uniting their two kingdoms into one country—Spain. Now they wanted everyone in that country to be Christian. They launched the Holy Inquisition, hunting down and prosecuting anyone considered a heretic, or a non-Christian believer. Jews were the main victims, but many others were persecuted and killed.

Expelled from Spain

In 1492, all Jews were banished from Spain. The king allowed them three months to settle their affairs and leave the country. When efforts to reverse the edict failed, about one hundred and twenty thousand Jews left Spain for countries including Portugal, Morocco, Italy, and Turkey. Although those who fled to Portugal were also targeted by the Inquisition, many of the expelled Jews survived. Descendents of these Jews are called *Sephardim,* from the Hebrew word for Spain.

About the Medieval Era

Historians date the medieval era from about the 400s to the 1400s. In some places, such as Japan, it lasted until the early 1800s while in others, such as Italy, it ended with the Renaissance in the late 1300s. It marked a point in world history that saw the rise of great kingdoms, the growth of international trade, and increased exploration. Many of the discoveries and advancements of the time became the foundation of our modern-day society. The word *medieval* refers to events, art, lifestyles, or architecture from that period.

Legend

Mayan pyramid. The Mayas built stepped pyramids for religious worship.

Chinese character. This symbol represents 'woman' in written Chinese.

Star and Crescent. The Star and Crescent is one of the most recognizable symbols of Islam.

Triple Horn of Odin. This symbol represents Odin, the father of the gods in Norse mythology.

Lion rampant. Lions were commonly used in medieval heraldry, symbolizing bravery, courage, and royalty.

Torii. These structures are found at the entrances of Shinto and Buddhist shrines across Japan.

Gold. Bags of gold dust were one of the main forms of currency in Mali.

Gondola. This boat is used to move people through Venice's canals. It dates back to at least the 1000s.

Star of David. The Star of David became a symbol for Judaism during the Middle Ages.

Credits

Care has been taken to trace ownership of copyright material contained in this book. Information enabling the publisher to rectify any reference or credit line in future editions will be welcomed.

PHOTOS: **Royalty-free Dreamstime: cover (background), 4–5, 14, 25, 45, 54, 65, 74, 94; Royalty-free iStockphoto: 34, 85**

ILLUSTRATIONS: **Peter Ferguson: cover, 1, 3, and all portraits; Colin McGill: all maps and spots**

CONSULTANTS: **Karen Bassie, University of Calgary; Deryck Brown, Vinland Viking Society; Brian A. Catlos, University of California Santa Cruz/University of Colorado at Boulder; Thomas D. Conlan, Bowdoin College; J. Michael Farmer, the University of Texas at Dallas; Abdul Nasser Kaadan, Aleppo University; Chris Kleinhenz, University of Wisconsin-Madison; Trevor H.J. Marchand, School of Oriental & African Studies; Geoff Rector, University of Ottawa; S. Alexander Takeuchi, University of North Alabama**

Thanks to John Crossingham, Larissa Byj, and Alicia Androich for all their help researching and editing this book.